Twelve military heroes.
Twelve indomitable heroines.
*One **UNIFORMLY HOT!** miniseries.*

Harlequin Blaze's bestselling miniseries
continues with another year of irresistible soldiers
from all branches of the armed forces.

Don't miss

ALL THE RIGHT MOVES
by Jo Leigh
June 2013

FREE FALL
by Karen Foley
July 2013

TO THE LIMIT
by Jo Leigh
August 2013

Uniformly Hot!
The Few. The Proud. The Sexy as Hell.

Available wherever Harlequin books are sold.

D0172370

Blaze®

Dear Reader,

For years, I've been fascinated by Whidbey Island, located in Puget Sound, just a few hours from Seattle. I've worked with many people who've been stationed at the naval air base there, and they all spoke of the beauty of the island and the surrounding area.

Two summers ago, I finally had the opportunity to visit Whidbey Island myself. I spent ten days exploring the quaint fishing villages, the miles of beaches, quiet coves and trails. Like my heroine, Maggie, I hiked down to the rocky beach below the Deception Pass Bridge and watched the navy pilots perform training maneuvers in the skies over those churning waters.

I knew then that I wanted to write a story set in this magical place, where a local girl falls hopelessly in love with one of these pilots, but believes the mistakes of her past will prevent them from having a future together. Thankfully, my hero, Jack Callahan, is a guy who always signs up for the difficult missions!

I hope you enjoy reading Maggie and Jack's story as they both search for where they belong, and that you'll fall in love with them—and Whidbey Island— the way I did.

Happy reading!

Karen Foley

Free Fall

—

Karen Foley

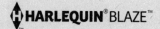
HARLEQUIN® BLAZE™

Recycling programs
for this product may
not exist in your area.

ISBN-13: 978-0-373-79761-5

FREE FALL

Printed in U.S.A.

ABOUT THE AUTHOR

Karen Foley is an incurable romantic. When she's not working for the Department of Defense, she's writing sexy romances with strong heroes and happy endings. She lives in Massachusetts with her husband and two daughters, an overgrown puppy and two very spoiled cats. Karen enjoys hearing from her readers. You can find out more about her by visiting www.karenefoley.com.

Books by Karen Foley

HARLEQUIN BLAZE

This book is dedicated to my dad, Byron Reynolds,
a navy veteran and the best father
a girl could ever want.
Thanks, Dad!

1

MAGNIFICENT.

There was simply no other word to describe him.

"Oh, man, you are so freaking gorgeous," Maggie Copeland breathed in appreciation. "So strong and sleek. C'mon, show me what you've got…give it to me, baby."

It had been years since she'd seen a male specimen as thrilling as this one, and she'd almost forgotten how the sight could make her heart race and her blood sing. As if sensing he had an eager audience, the orca breached, lifting his entire body out of the water and twisting upward in a glorious show of strength and grace, before falling back into the waves. Maggie gasped in admiration. Shamu had nothing on this beauty.

Her fingers worked quickly on the shutter release, snapping pictures in rapid succession. High overhead, she could barely hear the traffic on the twin bridges that spanned the narrow strait known as Deception Pass and connected Whidbey Island to the mainland. But she knew if she looked up, she would see the tiny shapes of hundreds of tourists who had pulled off the road to glimpse the killer whale as he frolicked in the frigid waters below the bridge.

Maggie almost hadn't bothered to stop, but her curiosity had gotten the best of her. Well, that and the fact that she'd been looking for any excuse to delay reaching her destination. After pulling over, she'd attached a telephoto lens to her camera and had made her way along the pedestrian walkway of the soaring bridge. Her first peek over the edge had made her head swim, and she'd pulled quickly back, her heart racing. The drop was dizzying, and it had taken several moments before she'd had the courage to take a second look, telling herself she wasn't afraid of heights. But when she'd glimpsed the orca some two hundred feet below, she'd forgotten everything except her desire to capture the magnificent animal on film.

She'd been a teenager the last time she'd navigated the steep, rocky trail that twisted its way beneath the bridge to the water's edge. Even then, with her brother beside her, she'd been terrified of falling, but tonight she'd managed the descent effortlessly, despite the fading light and the weight of the heavy lens bumping against her hip. The fragrant scent of crushed pine needles underfoot, combined with the salty ocean air, had been so familiar that for a brief moment she'd felt a wave of nostalgia. She hadn't been back to the Pacific Northwest in almost ten years, and she'd forgotten how good the Puget Sound air smelled. Now she crouched on a high rock overlooking the turbulent waters of Deception Pass, with an unobstructed view of the orca. If only she had more daylight!

Lowering the camera, she glanced toward the horizon, where the sun was rapidly slipping away beneath a breathtaking display of purple-and-orange-streaked sky. In another minute, it would disappear completely. The few people who had joined her on the rocky shoreline were already making their way back up to the road, leaving her alone. If she didn't start back to her car now, she'd have a difficult time negotiating the trail in the dark. She might not be anxious to return to her childhood home in the tiny community of Rocks Village, but neither did she relish the thought of spending the night on a deserted beach.

With a last, longing look at the orca, almost invisible now except for the tall, black fin that sliced through the water, Maggie secured her camera over one shoulder and carefully began working her way to the ground. Almost immediately, her fear of heights returned and she realized that getting down from the boulder was not going to be as easy as climbing up had been. What had earlier seemed a manageable height now seemed like a frightening drop to the rocky beach.

In an instant, she was fifteen years old again, excited that her brother and his friends had allowed her to come with them to Whistle Lake on neighboring Anacortes Island. The twenty-foot cliffs were popular with the local kids as a place to prove their bravery and cool off during the warm summer months. But Eric and his friends had craved bigger thrills, and had instead hiked to where the cliffs towered fifty to sixty feet high over the lake. One by one, they had leapt from the rocks into the deep water, and then taunted Maggie when she'd refused to join them.

Nothing could have induced her to leave the security of that rock, but she hadn't seen Eric's friend, who had climbed out of the water, make his way stealthily back to where she stood. With a cry of triumph, he had rushed at her. Although later he claimed that he'd only meant to give her a scare, he'd barreled into her, plunging them both over the edge. Maggie knew she'd been fortunate to have only broken a leg, and the boys had been lucky that her mother hadn't killed them. Maggie had never been back to Whistle Lake and avoided heights whenever she could.

Now, working her fingers into a crack in the surface of the stone, she clung to the side and searched for her next foothold, but there was none. Peering down, she wondered if she could jump, but quickly decided against it. The rocks made the option too dangerous, and she didn't want to risk breaking an ankle or, worse, damaging her precious camera.

Wishing she was wearing jeans and not a pair of shorts, Maggie stretched her leg downward, feeling blindly for a place to set her foot, and scraped her bare knee against the rough surface of the stone. Swearing softly, she finally succeeded in finding a small sliver of ledge. With her weight now balanced, she groped for a new handhold, dismayed when her camera strap slid from her shoulder and down the length of her arm to her wrist. Nudged off balance by the weight of the heavy lens, she made a grab for it, but it slipped free of her fingers. Instinctively, she stuck her foot out and snagged the strap with her foot. Maggie winced as the camera dangled precariously from the toe of her sneaker, and the telephoto lens bounced sickeningly against the hard stone.

Crap. Now what? She clung to the rock with both hands, balanced on an outcropping no wider than her thumb, with one leg stuck out at a precarious angle and her expensive camera swinging from her foot.

"Do you need a hand?"

Startled, Maggie nearly lost her footing. The voice

was deep, masculine and unless she was mistaken, amused. She hadn't heard anyone approaching, and now she carefully craned her head to get a look at the newcomer. A man stood directly below her with his arms raised as if to catch her. Even from her height, she could see he was young and good-looking, and his voice had a quality that caused something to resonate deep inside her.

"Uh…okay."

He stepped forward, and this time she heard the crunch of rocks beneath his feet. "Here, let me take your camera, and then I can help you down."

Uncertainty washed over Maggie. She'd spent a small fortune on the camera, and even more on the telephoto lens. These two pieces of equipment were all she had brought with her from Chicago, yet they constituted the foundation of her photography business. If this guy decided to do a grab-and-run, she'd be completely screwed. But the decision was taken out of her hands when he reached up and removed the camera strap from her foot and casually slid it over one shoulder.

"Careful," she admonished, keeping a sharp eye on him in case he should decide to bolt.

"No worries," he said easily. "Now it's your turn."

To Maggie's horror and astonishment, he reached up and put his hands on the back of her bare calves, gripping them firmly. Part of her realized that he was only trying to help, but his touch seemed to scorch her skin, and it was all she could do not to jerk away.

"Okay, thank you," she replied, and her voice sounded high and breathless. "I can manage from here."

"There's another ledge about eight inches below you," he said, ignoring her words. "I'll help you find it."

With one hand wrapped around her leg, he eased it

slowly downward until Maggie found the small toehold. "Great, I've got this," she assured him, not at all sure that she did. "Thanks."

"Are you experienced at bouldering?" Now there was no mistaking the amusement in his voice.

"At what?" she asked, momentarily distracted.

"Never mind, I can see that you're not." Instead of stepping back, the man slid his big hands up to her hips. "You've run out of toeholds, sweetheart. Let go. I've got you."

With both hands gripping her hips, he plucked her from the side of the rock as if she weighed no more than a child. Maggie gave a small cry of surprise as she found herself in his arms, her hands clutching at his broad shoulders. Immediately, she was swamped with sensation.

He felt solid beneath her fingers, and he smelled incredible, like clean laundry and something spicy. Heat poured off of him, and she could feel it even through the layers of their clothing. She had an almost overwhelming urge to curl herself around him and absorb his warmth. He didn't immediately release her, and it didn't occur to Maggie to protest. Even in the darkness, she could feel the intensity of his stare. Was it her imagination, or did his arms tighten fractionally around her?

"I've got you," he repeated, and his voice sounded a little husky.

Suddenly, she became aware of the intimacy of their position. Her arms were still looped around his neck, and their faces were so close that she could feel his warm breath against her cheek. Something tightened inside her, making her feel unsettled and short of breath and, despite the cool breeze coming in off the ocean, much too warm. To her relief, he loosened his hold, allowing her to slide the length of his body until her feet touched the ground.

"Thank you," she gasped, stepping back. Her equilibrium was off, and she swayed. He put a hand out to steady her.

"Are you okay?"

Maggie nodded as she gaped up at him. He was tall, probably a few inches over six feet, and leanly muscled. He wore a white shirt with the sleeves rolled carelessly back over his forearms and a pair of cargo shorts. His hair was cut short, and there was no mistaking the humor in his expression.

"I'm fine," she assured him. "Just feeling a little foolish."

"Why? It could have happened to anyone," he assured her.

"But not to you," she guessed, smiling.

"Nope," he agreed, grinning shamelessly. "Not to me." He slid the strap from his shoulder and handed the camera to her, using one hand to support the telephoto lens. Once she had it back in her hands, she relaxed fractionally.

"Thank you. I don't know what I'd have done if you hadn't come along when you did."

And now that she was no longer in danger of being trapped on the boulder, or lying injured at the base of it, she realized they were alone on the narrow strip of beach, and the earlier glow of the sunset was deepening into the violet of nightfall. Waves washed against the rocky beach, sucking and dragging the stones back into the surf with a loose rattling sound. Maggie knew she should be nervous, but instead she felt oddly safe. Call her crazy, but there was something vaguely familiar about the man, although she was certain they had never met before. If anything, he kept a deliberate distance between them, as if sensing her apprehension.

"Did you get some good pictures?" he asked.

"Of the orca? Yes, I think so."

"I saw them briefly, from up above," he continued conversationally, "but by the time I got down here, they were gone."

"They?" she asked in surprise, momentarily forgetting her caution.

"Didn't you see? There were two of them: a male and a female. The first was here, in the strait. The female was headed toward the open sea."

"What makes you think it was a male and a female?"

He smiled, his teeth white in the darkness. "From the shape of the dorsal fin. The female has a smaller, curved fin. The male's fin is tall and straight."

Maggie knew enough about orcas to know he was right. *A male and a female.* How had she missed the female? Of course, she'd only been scanning the waters of the pass itself, and hadn't been looking toward the ocean. If a second killer whale had been swimming just beyond the headland, it was no wonder she hadn't spotted it.

She couldn't blame the female; faced with the choice of following the male into the narrow bay behind Whidbey Island or making a run for the open sea and freedom, she'd choose the latter, too.

She had chosen freedom, too, she reminded herself.

She'd left Whidbey Island, located north of Seattle in Puget Sound, nearly ten years ago, and she hadn't looked back. Chicago represented freedom to her, and everything she'd never had growing up on an island in the Pacific Northwest. More importantly, it offered an escape from the humiliating memories of what had happened ten years ago. So why didn't she feel like she belonged in Chicago? She'd tried to convince herself that the city was where her future lay, but it was times like this that she understood what she'd given up; there would be no killer whale sightings in Chicago, or the scent of salt-tinged air, or the breathtaking beauty of Deception Pass with the sun sinking behind the horizon. With an irritated sigh, she pushed her nostalgia aside, reminding herself that she was only here for three weeks. No way would she allow herself to be drawn back by the local charm and beauty of the area. So maybe Chicago wasn't where she belonged, but neither was Whidbey Island.

"Well, thanks for your help," she said politely, and indicated the trailhead that led back to the road. "I'm going to head back up."

He fell into step beside her, putting one hand beneath her elbow as the terrain grew steep. "You wouldn't want to fall," he said in explanation as she looked at him in surprise. "Not with that camera. Of course, I *could* carry it for you."

Even with the strap around her neck, Maggie kept one hand on the lens to prevent it from swinging. The result was that her balance was a little off. She considered him for a moment. He seemed sincere enough, and he *had* helped her. After a moment, she removed the strap from around her neck and handed the camera to him.

"If you're sure you don't mind…"

"I'm sure." He positioned the strap over his body, steadied the lens in one hand and indicated she should precede him up the trail. "After you."

Maggie clambered gracelessly up the steep path, acutely conscious of the man behind her. Was he checking out her butt? Could he even see her butt? Honestly, it was so dark she had trouble seeing the path. As they climbed higher, the pine trees around them grew thicker, and soon they were in dense woods and visibility was close to zero.

"Hold up a minute," he called from behind her.

Maggie paused and glanced over her shoulder. He was closer than she realized, and while her breathing was already labored from exertion, he wasn't even winded.

"Here, let me go first." Without waiting for her response, he stepped past her on the narrow path. "Take my hand."

Maggie was grateful for the darkness that hid her surprise and masked the flush of heat in her face and neck. Reaching out, she felt her hand warmly enclosed in his larger one.

"We'll take it nice and slow," he said, and Maggie could hear the smile in his voice.

As they made their way up the steep trail, she found herself grateful for his assistance. She stumbled twice and would have fallen if not for his steadying hand. By the time they reached the top, she was out of breath and her calves were cramping with effort.

"Are you okay?" he asked, releasing her hand.

They were in the parking lot, where at least a dozen cars were parked. Several tourists drifted toward them from the bridge.

Maggie dragged in a deep breath and nodded. "Yes, just a little winded."

Which was an understatement. She could barely catch her breath, and it had nothing to do with her recent exertions. For the first time, she had a good look at the stranger's face. A light pole near the visitor's center cast intriguing shadows over his features as he carefully removed her camera and handed it back to her. Maggie knew she was staring, but couldn't help herself. The guy was seriously hot. She guessed him to be in his early thirties, and he had the kind of open-faced friendliness that was hard, if not impossible, to resist. Strong, white teeth. A dent in one lean cheek that begged to be touched. A clean, square jawline. A mouth made for kissing.

Whoa. Where had *that* come from?

Maggie took an instinctive step backward, still staring at him. Yep. He was gorgeous, and she realized she wasn't immune to his good looks or the masculine interest reflected in his eyes. She could feel the tug of attraction like the insidious pull of an undertow, and there was a part of her that wanted to go with it, to let the current sweep her away.

"Well, thanks again," she said quickly, and turned toward her car.

"You're welcome." Instead of turning away, he walked across the parking lot beside her. "My rig's right over here," he said in explanation, when she cast him a questioning glance.

His *rig* was a dark Land Rover, an older model with four doors and a hard top. A large cargo box was secured to the roof, but Maggie could just as easily envision a kayak or a surfboard there instead. The guy oozed outdoor adventure. Through the rear windows of the vehicle, Maggie could see the back was packed with boxes and she found her curiosity piqued in spite of herself.

"Looks like you're going on a trip," she commented.

"Actually, my trip ends here. I just drove cross-country from Florida."

"Oh, wow. That's impressive." Maggie wasn't ex-aggerating. Her own drive from Chicago to Washington State had been long and exhausting. She couldn't imagine driving all the way from Florida. But she could picture him clearly in a pair of brightly colored board shorts, effortlessly riding a surfboard through turquoise waves. His body would be tanned and supremely fit, and the water would cause his skin to gleam....

Maggie gave herself a mental shake. She didn't know the first thing about this guy, and yet she couldn't prevent her imagination from conjuring up sexy images of him. They were next to her car, and Maggie bent to shake a small pebble out of her shoe, holding the camera steady with one hand. As she balanced on one foot, her stranger put a hand beneath her arm to steady her. She was acutely conscious of the warmth and strength of his fingers, and for a brief instant, imagined what it would be like to have a guy like him in her life; to know she could rely on him for anything, and that he would always be there to lend his support, like he was doing right now.

In the next instant, she dismissed the idea. Sure, he made her feel feminine and safe, but she didn't know the first thing about him. There was no reason for her to think he was the kind of guy who had staying power, or that he was even available. Besides, she wasn't in the market for a boyfriend, especially not one who had just moved to Whidbey Island. Not when she would return to Chicago in just three weeks.

Replacing her shoe, she stood upright, but he didn't immediately release her arm, and Maggie found herself swaying toward him. Was it her imagination, or did he apply a subtle pressure? Glancing at his face, she saw him staring at her mouth, and the expression in his eyes was so sexy that Maggie found herself momentarily transfixed.

Her breathing hitched.

In that instant, she knew he was going to kiss her, and she was going to let him. Call her crazy, but she wanted to know what his mouth would feel like on hers. The likelihood that she would ever see him again was slim to none. What harm could there be in a simple kiss? Besides, if it wasn't for him, she might still be trapped on that damned rock.

As if sensing her willingness, he bent his head fractionally, until their lips were almost touching.

"I'd really like to kiss you," he breathed.

In answer, Maggie pressed her mouth against his. The instant their lips met, heat flared between them. He bracketed her face in his hands, angling her head and fastening his mouth over hers in a soft, moist fusing that robbed her legs of strength and had her leaning helplessly into him. The guy knew how to kiss, and Maggie found herself welcoming the hot, sweet slide of his tongue against hers. Heat bloomed low in her abdomen and her blood sang in her ears. Without conscious thought, she pressed closer, seeking more of the intimate caress. The camera dug into her ribs, and she was unprepared when he released her and stepped abruptly away.

They stood staring at each other for several long seconds, their breathing uneven, until he turned away and scrubbed a hand over his face. Maggie's entire body throbbed with awareness, and when she traced her tongue experimentally over her lips, she could taste him there. Shaken, she cleared her throat and strove for a conversational tone, as if she hadn't just come within seconds of tearing his clothes off.

"So, what brings you to Whidbey Island?"

He whirled around and gave her a bemused look, as if he couldn't quite believe she was making small talk after that incredibly hot kiss. Maggie blinked at him and smiled politely. She'd been close enough to him to feel the muscles that layered his body. The guy had an incredible physique, and she felt sure that whatever had brought him to Whidbey Island involved doing something that provided a physical challenge. Based on the gear he had packed in his Land Rover, he planned on staying in the area for a while. Suddenly, the prospect of spending three weeks on Whidbey Island didn't seem quite so bad.

"My job," he finally replied. "I report for duty tomorrow morning at the naval air station."

Any lingering warmth from their shared kiss was doused by a cold wash of reality. Maggie was momentarily at a loss for words. She definitely hadn't seen that one coming.

"You're in the military?" Her voice sounded high and breathless.

"You bet."

An airman. Or a sailor. It didn't matter which; one was as bad as the other. Maggie almost sagged in disappointment, even as a small, inner voice mocked her. What had she thought? That she could meet some sexy stranger on a dark beach, fall madly in love and live happily ever after? *He was in the military.*

She should have known he was too good to be true. After all, her own father, a navy supply officer, had walked away from her mother when he'd learned she was pregnant with twins. And just to make sure Maggie hadn't missed the memo the first time around, the universe had sent her a second smack down. Ten years ago, the young navy officer she'd been engaged to had inexplicably dumped her in order to marry another woman.

Maggie took an involuntary step backward, putting a safe distance between them. She needed to turn and walk away. Away from him. Away from temptation. And she needed to do it now, before he did.

Because she knew from bitter experience that the one thing military guys were good at was leaving.

2

"So, you're sure you don't mind doing this?"

Maggie stood on the wide, covered veranda of the spacious Victorian where she had grown up, and gave her twin brother, Eric, a tolerant look. "Would I have come all the way from Chicago if I minded?"

Her brother ran his fingers through his hair in a distracted manner, causing it to stand on end. "I just know how much you hate Whidbey Island. But I wouldn't have asked you to come back if it wasn't important. Danielle and I really need this vacation."

"I know that. And I don't *hate* Whidbey Island," Maggie said cautiously. "I just outgrew it."

"It's been ten years, Maggie." Eric's expression was sympathetic. "I'll bet nobody even remembers what happened back then. Besides, none if it was your fault."

Maggie squinted, even though she stood well in the shade of the porch. There was no way she wanted to talk about what had happened all those years ago. For her, the memories were still too fresh.

Too humiliating.

Ignoring his words, she looked past Eric to where

her sister-in-law, Danielle, sat waiting for him in the car. "Look, you'd better go if you're going to catch your flight. Please don't worry about a thing. The house will be fine, and I'll have Carly to help me with the shop."

"And you're sure you can manage the festival?"

The annual arts-and-crafts festival in Coupeville was one of the biggest events of the summer months, drawing tourists from all over the greater northwest. Maggie's mother had created an exclusive line of sea-glass jewelry more than twenty years ago, and what had begun as a hobby and a way to make a little extra money had grown into a lucrative family business. Maggie had grown up helping her mom run a tent at the festival every summer until she'd turned eighteen, and knew she would have no problem running a tent for her brother. Both Eric and his wife were talented artists who had taken the line of sea-glass jewelry to a whole new level. They frequently traveled to South America and Europe to collect their sea glass, although Eric had found some of his rarest pieces of glass right on the nearby beaches of Puget Sound. In addition to their small shop, Village Sea Glass, in downtown Coupeville, they had a thriving online business, and their work had been featured in numerous upscale magazines.

And if Maggie did have any reservations, Carly Bates was there to help her. Carly helped Eric run his shop, and was a well-known glass artist on Whidbey Island. She'd been attending the annual arts festival for longer than Maggie had been alive.

Now she resisted rolling her eyes at her brother and gave him a cheerful smile instead.

"I'll be fine. You and Danielle go and have fun… it may be the last vacation you have for a long time."

Eric's wife was six months' pregnant with twins, and

they'd decided to take a long-anticipated trip to Hawaii to visit her parents while she could still travel. Normally, Maggie and Eric's mother would step in and run the jewelry shop that Eric owned in downtown Coupeville, as well as help out at the festival. But this year she had opted to spend the summer in California with her boyfriend. At forty-eight years old, Valerie Copeland was finally enjoying life away from Whidbey Island. Maggie was happy for her. How could either she or Eric ask her to sacrifice anything else for them? It was the only reason that Maggie had agreed to come back to Whidbey Island—so her mother wouldn't have to.

Eric gave her a grateful smile. "Thanks, sis, you're the best. You have my number if you need to reach me."

"I'll be fine, now go!"

Eric bounded down the porch steps and then stopped halfway down the walk and turned, smacking a hand to his head. "Geez, I almost forgot!"

Maggie waited expectantly.

Her brother actually looked embarrassed. "There's a new tenant moving into the cottage, but I haven't had a chance to clean the place up after the last guy left."

Their mother had inherited the gracious Victorian overlooking the waters of Penn Cove when Eric and Maggie were twelve years old. Their grandparents had once operated a bed-and-breakfast out of the house, and had rented the small cottage on the property to vacationing families. After they had passed away, Valerie Copeland had turned the Victorian back into a private home and had opted to rent the cottage on a long-term basis, mostly to struggling artists. The small house had a stunning view of the water, and Valerie had added heat for the winter and a deck on the back for enjoyment in the warmer months. As a teenager, Maggie had watched numerous artists transfer in and out of the cottage, and she knew the drill.

"It's fine," she assured her brother. "I'll give the place a good cleaning. When is the new tenant due to arrive?"

"Not for a couple of weeks," Eric said quickly.

Unbidden, an image of the guy from the previous night flashed through Maggie's head. She'd lain awake for most of the night thinking about him, replaying their kiss over and over again in her head. Realistically, she knew the likelihood of seeing him again before she returned to Chicago was slim to none. The naval air station was located about fifteen miles from the small community of Rocks Village, in the town of Oak Harbor. She'd have to drive completely around Penn Cove and then head to the northern end of the island in order to reach the base. Even then, he probably didn't live in the town of Oak Harbor, but on the air base itself, behind the guarded gates and barbed wire fences, making the chances of another encounter even more unlikely. She told herself that it was for the best.

With a mental shake, she dragged her thoughts away from the stranger. They only ever rented the cottage to artists, and Maggie wondered briefly what medium the new tenant might specialize in. Hopefully not moose droppings, like the artist who had stayed in the cottage the year Maggie had turned sixteen. "Okay, I've got it covered," she assured her brother. "*Now go,* before you miss your flight!"

Eric sprinted toward the car. He blew Maggie a quick kiss as he climbed behind the wheel. "Thanks, Maggie. You're the best!"

Maggie watched the car until it disappeared down the long gravel drive. Closing the door, she leaned against it and stared around her at the familiar rooms where she'd spent her childhood. By all accounts, it had been a good childhood, even without a father to complete their family. Valerie had been an artist and a single mom, but had always put her two small children first. And during the times when she had been working, Maggie's grandparents had cared for them, ensuring both she and Eric were spoiled rotten. So why did coming home fill her with such anxiety?

JACK CALLAHAN DREW his Land Rover to a stop on the side of the narrow road and double-checked the address he'd scribbled on a piece of paper, before glancing again at the mailbox. This was it, and if he'd had any doubts, they were squelched by the small Cottage for Rent sign that had been pushed into the ground beside the mailbox. Thrusting the Land Rover into Drive, he turned down the gravel road. Dense trees pressed in on both sides of the long road, but through the foliage he caught shimmering glimpses of water.

The private drive was long, winding its way through the trees until they suddenly fell away to reveal a large Victorian house with a wraparound porch. A center turret dominated the roofline and Jack was certain it provided unobstructed views of Penn Cove. Parking the Land Rover, he took the porch steps two at a time and knocked on the door, but there was no answer. Walking to the end of the porch, he surveyed the property, with its lush gardens and gravel walkways. There was no sign of life, but he could hear the faint strains of music coming from somewhere toward the back of the house.

Leaving the porch, Jack followed a narrow path through the yard until he came to a guesthouse perched on a small knoll. The cottage was quaint without being fussy, and a stone chimney on one end gave it some substance. The roof overhung the door and windows, which all stood wide open. Music came from inside, and now he could hear a woman's voice singing along, completely out of tune.

Jack knocked on the open door, but the woman's voice continued singing. He stepped inside and found himself in a roomy living area dominated by a stone fireplace at one end, furnished with a comfortable sofa, an oversized coffee table and a couple of sturdy end tables. Following the music, he entered a small kitchen and stopped short.

A woman lay on her back on the floor, with her upper body concealed inside a cupboard beneath the small sink. On the floor around her lay an assortment of wrenches and screwdrivers. A radio on top of the counter blared pop music, and she interrupted her lusty singing just long enough to release a string of colorful curses, before picking up the lyrics again.

Jack grinned, and let his eyes travel the length of her body. She wore a pair of white shorts and her legs were pale, but toned. And right now they were spread wide, sandaled feet planted firmly on the wooden floor as she wrestled with the plumbing. Jack tried not to stare at her crotch, but couldn't prevent his gaze from lingering on the strip of pale skin above the waistband of her shorts, where her T-shirt had ridden up, or the soft thrust of her breasts beneath the thin cotton.

"Excuse me," he said, loudly enough for her to hear him over the music.

Her body stilled, and then she slid out from beneath the sink to a sitting position on the floor. Surprise was slowly replaced by an expression of shocked recognition, and Jack felt his own mouth drop open, before he quickly snapped it shut.

"You." Her voice was little more than a whisper.

She scrambled to her feet, and Jack automatically extended a hand to help her. She was the same woman he'd met on the beach two nights ago; the same one who'd retreated to her car so fast after he'd kissed her that he hadn't even gotten her name. But that hadn't prevented him from thinking about that kiss over the next couple of days, and wondering who she was. He couldn't believe she was here, in the cottage he'd rented for the next several months.

"Do you own this property?" He couldn't keep the astonishment out of his voice. Jack didn't believe in coincidences, but what were the chances of them meeting again like this?

She swiped her hands self-consciously on the seat of her shorts, drawing his attention to her round bottom, and causing the fabric of her T-shirt to stretch taut over her full breasts. In the daylight, she was even prettier than he remembered, with eyes the color of the Pacific, and coppery red hair. She'd pulled the unruly mass back into a ponytail, but several tendrils had come loose and clung damply to her neck. But it was her mouth that really caught his attention. Her lips were full and soft, the upper lip pillowy plump. Jack recalled how they'd felt when he'd kissed her, and had to drag his thoughts away from that dangerous territory.

She wasn't beautiful in the traditional sense, but there was an untamed quality about her that appealed to him. Right now, she looked like she might bolt if he gave her half a chance. He watched as she switched off the radio, plunging the cottage into silence. His own heartbeat drummed loudly in his ears.

"My mother does. At least, she used to. She gave the house to my brother when he got married." She was staring at him now, her expression a mixture of wariness and curiosity. "What are you doing here? How did you find me?"

Jack frowned, and then her meaning dawned on him. "You think I've been looking for you?" He couldn't keep the amusement out of his voice. He *had* thought of her, probably more than was healthy, considering he knew nothing about her, but she gave him more credit than he deserved if she thought he'd deliberately tracked her down.

Seeing his expression, a wash of color stained her cheeks, and she brushed past him and stepped out onto a small deck on the back of the cottage. Jack followed her. She braced her hands on the railing of the deck and breathed deeply before angling her head to look at him.

"I'm sorry, but what was I supposed to think?" Her tone was defensive. "I meet a complete stranger on the beach, exchange one hot kiss and then lo and behold, he shows up on my doorstep. It was a natural conclusion."

Jack shrugged. "I don't know. Maybe I'm here because I've rented the cottage."

She turned and stared at him in disbelief. "What? That's impossible. My brother said the new tenant wouldn't be here for a couple of weeks. Besides, we only ever rent this place to local artists, never to military guys." She ran a critical eye over him. "No matter how gorgeous they might be."

Jack bit back a smile, and rubbed the bridge of his nose. So she thought he was gorgeous, did she?

"I met your brother a couple of months ago when I came out here on a house-hunting trip. He offered me the cottage and I accepted. My original reporting date wasn't until next month, but I got released from my last assignment a couple of weeks early, and made good time driving out here."

"Oh."

He extended his hand. "I'm Jack Callahan."

Almost reluctantly, she took his hand. "Maggie Copeland."

Her touch caused a lick of heat along his arm, and he had an insane urge to drag her up against his body and kiss her the way he had the other night. Maybe he'd only imagined the inferno that simmered just beneath the surface, but somehow, he didn't think so. He pulled his hand back quickly, in case he actually acted on the impulse. "Do you have a plumbing problem?" he asked, hoping she didn't notice his odd behavior.

"What? Oh, yes. There's a leak in the pipe, but I think I fixed it."

"I'm pretty handy, and I can take care of any maintenance issues with the cottage. I don't expect you—or your brother—to do that."

"How, exactly, did you and my brother meet?"

He could hear the skepticism in her voice, and it was clear she found it difficult to believe that her brother had rented the cottage to him.

"I came out here a couple of months ago on a house-hunting trip, but didn't have much success finding a place to live. The last day on the island, I was looking for a souvenir and walked into a little shop in Coupeville. I met the owner—your brother. He and I got talking and the rest, as they say, is history. That was back in March. I'm surprised he didn't say something to you."

Maggie averted her gaze." Yeah, well, I live in Chicago. I'm only here for a few weeks while he and his wife are on vacation."

Jack felt a stab of disappointment at hearing she didn't live locally. He hadn't planned on getting involved with anyone, but now that their paths had crossed twice, he couldn't deny that he wanted to see more of Maggie. He wanted a repeat performance of the parking-lot encounter. Hell, he wanted *her*. He couldn't recall the last time he'd been so turned on by a simple kiss, and he acknowledged that everything about Maggie Copeland appealed to him, from the sweet curve of her ass beneath the white shorts, to her prickly attitude. But a few weeks wasn't very much time to get her to warm up to him, and if she was heading back to Chicago, the effort might well be pointless.

She squinted up at him. "Can I ask what you're paying for rent?"

He shrugged and told her the amount, but was unprepared when her eyes widened in shock.

"Are you kidding me?" She sounded horrified. "I mean, have you seen this place?"

She thought he was taking advantage of her brother. "I know," he said, raising both hands to stem her flow of words. "I think it's too low, too, but it's the maximum amount that the navy will allow."

She waved a hand in dismissal. "No, that's not what I mean. You're paying almost triple what we normally get from tenants. It's too much." She gestured around her. "I mean, look at this place."

Jack laughed softly, liking her even more. "Trust me, I have. It's perfect—exactly what I want."

Maggie gave him a dubious look. "Wouldn't you rather be in Oak Harbor? That's where most of the military live. In nice condos, close to the base, or the ocean."

Jack shrugged. "I'm with the guys in my squadron for ten to fourteen hours every day. I wanted to find a place outside of Oak Harbor, and this has everything I need. I used to spend time here when I was a kid, and I couldn't wait to get back."

For just a moment, he allowed himself to go back to his youth, when he'd spent summers with his grandparents on Whidbey Island. His grandfather had operated a whale-watching charter business, and Jack's happiest memories were of days spent on the waters of Puget Sound, trolling the orca feeding grounds in the hopes of sighting the magnificent animals.

Maggie made a snorting sound of disbelief, snapping Jack out of his reverie. Her voice was filled with disbelief. "You came back here voluntarily?"

"Actually, I did. I had a choice of several different assignments, but I chose Whidbey Island. You sound surprised."

She shrugged. "I just don't understand why anyone would want to live here on a permanent basis. Sure, it's beautiful, but when you see it on a daily basis, day in and day out, you become immune to it. You take it for granted."

"I don't think I'd ever take true beauty for granted," Jack said quietly.

Maggie gave him a sharp look, as if she suspected him of being insincere. "Trust me, after a while, you won't even notice the scenery. What you will notice is how isolated the island is. And unless you're in the military, there are very few worthwhile jobs." She gave a soft laugh. "But it sounds like you already knew all that before you decided to come back here, right? And you've obviously got the job thing figured out, so you should be very happy."

Giving him a bright smile, she turned and went back into the cottage. Jack followed her, turning her words over in his head. So she didn't like Whidbey Island, and she didn't like men in uniform. He'd gathered that much from the way she'd practically run from him after that sizzling kiss in the parking lot. Jack gave a rueful grin. Call him nuts, but he always had preferred the difficult missions to the easy ones. Now he had just a few short weeks in which to change her mind about the island—and about him.

3

MAGGIE TRIED TO ignore the new tenant, but found herself standing at her bedroom window and looking across the backyard to where lights glowed softly from inside the guesthouse. If she'd had any doubts that Jack Callahan really did intend to rent the small cottage, they'd been dispelled by the moving truck that had arrived the following day. Maggie had hovered near the back door of the main house, watching with interest as Jack worked alongside the movers to carry items into the cottage. He'd worn a T-shirt that had emphasized the broad thrust of his shoulders, and even from a distance she'd seen—and admired—the impressive bulge of his biceps.

He traveled light, and the movers had departed within an hour of their arrival. But Maggie had felt a sense of smug satisfaction that she hadn't been completely wrong about the guy—she'd spotted a surfboard among the items carried out of the van. But then Jack had wheeled a low-slung motorcycle out of the back of the truck and parked it beside the cottage. She hadn't expected that, but she could easily envision him on the bike.

Disgusted by the enjoyment she was getting from spying on him, Maggie determinedly left the house and had spent the remainder of the day at her brother's jewelry shop in Coupeville, the small waterfront town just a few miles down the road. But even with the distraction of the tourists who came in to browse in the shop, and Carly's constant chatter about the upcoming arts-and-crafts festival, Maggie had found her thoughts wandering back to the cottage, and the man who now lived there.

Even now she couldn't seem to drag her gaze from the guesthouse. A movement at the door of the cottage captured her attention, and she peered more closely through the window. It was Jack, and he was walking along the path that led to the main house. For a brief instant, she allowed herself to admire his loose-limbed, rolling gait, before panic galvanized her into action.

Jumping away from the window, she did a quick self-assessment. She was wearing a pair of loose pajama bottoms and a camisole top; she looked quickly around for something else to put on, but there was no time. She heard him knocking. Smoothing her hand over her hair, she made her way quickly down the stairs and through the kitchen to the back door, opening it wide.

Jack stood on the porch, looking even better than she remembered in a pair of jeans that were comfortably worn in all the right places, and hugged his package in a way that made it impossible for her not to notice. But when she forced her gaze upward, his faded T-shirt only emphasized the planes of his muscular chest and shoulders. Maggie swallowed hard. Maybe she really had gone too long without sex because looking at him now, that was all she could think of. Thankfully, he didn't seem to notice her blatant perusal of him.

In fact, he looked mildly irritated, but smiled when he saw her. His gaze briefly swept over her skimpy clothing, and Maggie didn't miss the flare of awareness in his eyes. She resisted the urge to cross her arms over her chest, feeling exposed and vulnerable.

"I hope I didn't wake you up," he began. "I saw a light on.…"

"No," Maggie said quickly. "I was just getting ready for bed."

"Well, I'm sorry to bother you, but I was hoping you had a wrench that I could borrow. The sink sprung another leak, and I can't find my tools in the boxes I brought with me."

"Oh, I'm so sorry. I thought I had fixed it yesterday." She turned away and quickly located the small toolbox that Eric kept in a closet. "I can come over and take another look at it."

Jack took the toolbox from her, and Maggie could see the amusement in his eyes. "I thought you were getting ready for bed?"

She had a sudden image of herself, lounging back on a sumptuous bed wearing nothing but a smile, waiting for him. "I was," she admitted, flushing, "but I don't mind coming over to take a look at your plumbing."

He laughed, but there was an expression in his eyes that caused something to unfurl low in Maggie's stomach. "I think that's supposed to be my line," he said with a grin, before sobering. "Thanks, but I've got it. You go to bed. Tomorrow, I'll head into town and pick up parts to replace the piping."

Maggie chewed her lip. She knew Eric wouldn't want his new tenant performing the plumbing work himself, and there was a part of her that was reluctant to see him leave. She liked his company. She liked the warm timbre of his voice, and the way he looked at her. And as much as she hated to admit it, she liked the way he made her feel, sort of shivery and hot all at the same time. "Really, you don't need to do that. I can take a look at it."

But he was already turning away and making his way back down the steps. "Thanks anyway," he called over his shoulder, "but I don't mind."

Slipping her feet into a pair of flip-flops and snagging a hoodie from a hook near the door, Maggie followed him along the path, pulling the sweatshirt over her head as she walked. "Look, you're paying enough in rent that you shouldn't have to do your own home repairs. Eric has a friend in town that does plumbing work. I'll call him first thing in the morning."

They had reached the cottage, and Jack opened the door, standing back to let Maggie enter. Stepping into the kitchen, she saw he'd mopped up the leak with several bath towels, and had unsuccessfully attempted to tighten the leaky joint with a variety of kitchen utensils, including a pair of tongs. Even now, a thin trickle of water seeped out of the cupboard and onto the floor.

Maggie automatically bent to wipe up the moisture, but found herself prevented from doing so by a strong hand on her arm.

"Leave it." Jack's voice was firm. "I didn't come up to the house because I expected you to come back and clean up for me. I can do that."

Even through the thin fabric of the hoodie, his hand was warm on her arm, and just like before, his touch seemed to scorch her. Releasing her, Jack set the toolbox on the counter and rummaged through the contents until he found a wrench.

"What can I do to help?" Maggie asked.

He nodded toward the refrigerator. "Grab a couple of beers and make yourself comfortable. This won't take long."

Maggie did as he asked, uncapping the bottles and handing one to Jack. He took it with a murmur of thanks, and Maggie watched with interest as he took a long swallow before setting the beer on the counter beside the toolbox. As she had done the day before, Jack lay on his back and slid his upper body into the open space beneath the sink, uncaring of the water that pooled beneath him.

"Hand me that wrench, would you?"

Maggie handed him the wrench and then crouched beside him, telling herself that she was only trying to be helpful, and that she wasn't ogling the taut muscles of his abdomen, exposed where his shirt had ridden up.

"Do you have enough light?" she asked, peering to where he was expertly tightening the pipe.

"There are some things that you don't need to see what you're doing in order to do them right," he replied smoothly.

Immediately, Maggie's imagination surged. He'd be an expert with a woman's body, knowing exactly where and how to touch her, and using more than just his hands. Stifling a groan, she took a hefty swig of beer.

"There." Jack let out a soft grunt of effort as he gave the wrench one last twist. "That'll do, at least until I can replace the pipe."

He eased himself out from beneath the sink and rose to his feet. Water soaked the back of his shirt and jeans, but she was unprepared when he reached behind his head and dragged the wet garment off.

Instantly, all the moisture in Maggie's mouth evaporated.

The guy was layered in muscle, from the contoured planes of his impressive pecs to the cobblestoned terrain of his abdomen. His skin was tanned and his chest was lightly dusted with soft hair that narrowed to an enticing trail over his flat stomach, then disappeared beneath the waistband of his jeans. Oblivious to her hungry gaze, he balled up the shirt and used it to wipe himself dry.

As Maggie continued to stare, slack-jawed, he seemed to recall himself. "Excuse me," he muttered. "I'll just go change." He strode from the room, and then ducked his head back through the kitchen door to flash a smile. "Don't go anywhere."

Maggie blew out a hard breath. The guy was seriously hot. Like center-of-the-sun hot. She took a gulp of her beer, and then pressed the cold bottle against her throat, letting the condensation cool her overheated skin. She should leave; she should go back up to the main house right now and try to forget the sight of his lean, hard body—and her own reaction to him. In fact, she should go back to Chicago, because she was suddenly certain that two thousand miles should be enough distance between them for her to resist the temptation he presented.

He returned almost immediately, tugging a clean T-shirt into place, and covering all that gorgeous maleness. Maggie wanted to weep with disappointment.

He looked suddenly uncertain, as if he wasn't sure what to do with her now that the plumbing issue had been taken care of. Maggie had a few explicit ideas, but decided she lacked the courage to suggest them. She set her bottle of beer down on the counter. "I should go."

For just an instant, she thought she saw regret on his face, before he schooled his expression into one of politeness. "I'll walk you back to the house."

"You don't need to do that; it's barely a hundred yards from here," she protested.

Jack shrugged. "Call me old-fashioned. It doesn't seem right to let you walk back by yourself in the dark."

"Okay, then." Maggie nodded, but couldn't prevent the small rush of pleasure she felt in knowing that he wanted to ensure her safety.

He opened the screen door of the cottage and stood back to let her pass. In the narrow confines of the doorway, she brushed up against him and couldn't help but notice how he stiffened at the contact. Was it possible that he was as aware of her as she was of him?

Outside, the night air was cool and filled with the sound of crickets and night bugs. Jack's booted feet crunched softly on the gravel path as he fell into step beside her.

"So what do you do out in Chicago?" he asked.

"Photography."

"Of course. I mean, I should have guessed. Do you have your own studio?"

"Not yet, but I'm working on it. I went to photography school out there, and then worked for a magazine for a couple of years, mostly shooting food items." She gave a soft laugh. "I had to get out of that business, because everything I photographed made me hungry! I'd probably weigh a million pounds if I'd stayed in that job."

"So what kind of photography do you do now?"

Maggie couldn't prevent a grimace. "Sadly, I do a lot of weddings."

Jack stopped walking, and even in the indistinct light, she could sense his curiosity. "Why sadly? I'd think wedding photography would be very…I don't know—uplifting, I guess. If you don't enjoy it, why do it?"

"It's not that," she protested woodenly. "I enjoy the work. But there are times I wonder if the bride is really getting the happy-ever-after that she's been dreaming about. Sometimes I think the glitz and glamour of the wedding day is like putting rouge on a corpse—it might look healthy to the casual observer, but when you wipe away the makeup, there's no life there."

Now there was no mistaking his surprise. Embarrassed that she'd revealed so much, Maggie turned and began walking determinedly toward the house. She glanced at him as he fell into step beside her. He probably thought she was bitter about weddings because she was still single. Because everyone knew that a woman couldn't possibly be happy unless she had a man in her life. And here she was, approaching thirty and not a prospect in sight.

"I'm sure not all wedding bells have the ring of doom," he finally said, a hint of laughter in his voice. "What about your brother? The last time I saw him, he seemed genuinely happy—a pretty wife, a baby on the way, a business he can be proud of. I'd say he's found his happy-ever-after."

Maggie nodded, wanting to change the subject. "You're right. Eric and Danielle are crazy about each other." She gave him a bright smile. "Don't listen to me, I'm just having a bad day."

"Oh, yeah?" They had reached her back door and stood facing each other under the entry light. "What made it so difficult?"

You. Having you so close.

She almost blurted the words out loud, but instead

shook her head and looked out beyond the dark yard, toward the water.

"Nothing I can explain. Maybe it's just being back here."

"How long has it been?"

"Almost ten years."

He was silent for a long moment, and she knew her words had shocked him. "So you were, what, just a teenager when you left?"

She tipped her chin up and looked directly at him. "I was almost nineteen. Old enough to be married."

He blanched. "Were you? Married?"

If he was going to be living in the tiny enclave of Rocks Village, then he would eventually learn the truth. Ten years wasn't nearly enough time for the locals to have forgotten what happened. But there was no way she was going to fill him in on the sordid details. She'd endured enough humiliation at being jilted; the last thing she wanted was this man's pity.

"I came close," she finally said. "But we didn't go through with it."

"Because you realized there was no life under the rouge?"

Oh, there was life, she thought bitterly, at least for her so-called fiancé. Another life, with another woman, whom she hadn't known existed.

"Something like that," she murmured.

"So you ran, and you didn't look back."

Maggie looked sharply at him, startled by his astuteness. "My leaving had nothing to do with that," she fibbed. "I simply decided to pursue my dream of becoming a photographer."

"In Chicago."

"Yes."

His lips quirked in a half smile, and the expression in his eyes was so understanding that for a moment, Maggie was tempted to tell him everything.

"What about now?"

She stared at him blankly. "What do you mean?"

"Is there someone waiting for you back in Chicago?"

Maggie thought briefly about the men in her life. There was Ramon, who had worked with her at the foodie magazine and who occasionally helped her out with her wedding assignments, but who was crazy about his partner, Kenny. Then there was Adam, the sweet old man who lived across the hall and brought her a plate of homemade cookies every Sunday afternoon. But she couldn't say that either of them was waiting anxiously for her return.

She shook her head. "No. There's nobody like that in Chicago."

"Good."

And just like that, the air between them thrummed with energy. Jack took a step toward her and Maggie held her breath. There was something in his expression—something hot and full of promise—that made her heart thump heavily against her ribs, and heat to slide beneath her skin. She couldn't remember the last time a man had made her feel so aware of herself as a woman. Reaching out, he traced a finger along her cheek.

"It's getting late. You should go to bed." His voice was low and Maggie thought it sounded strained.

Erotic images of the two of them, naked and entwined beneath her sheets, flashed through her mind. She should have her head examined for even considering getting involved with this man, yet every cell in her body ached for him. She recalled again how he had looked without his shirt on, all thrusting shoulders and sleek, hard muscle. But more than that, it had been the expression in his eyes that made it impossible for her to stop thinking about him. It had been years since she'd had a one-night stand, but she realized she wanted to know what it would be like to have his hands and mouth on her, to hear the sounds he would make as she brought him pleasure.

In three weeks, she would return to Chicago, and the likelihood of ever seeing Jack Callahan again was zero. Did she have the guts to reach out and take what she wanted, knowing she couldn't keep it? She wasn't sure, and suddenly she didn't care.

Turning, she opened the back door to the house, and then looked at Jack. "Why don't you join me?"

4

FOR A MOMENT, Jack was too stunned to react. He'd been consumed with lusty thoughts of her since he'd first seen her sprawled beneath the kitchen sink in the cottage. Earlier, when he'd pulled off his shirt, he'd caught the greedy expression on her face. He'd gone instantly hard and had fled the room before he'd done something he knew he'd regret later. But even after he'd changed his shirt and had come back into the room, the tension in the air had been palpable.

More than anything, he wanted to follow her to her bedroom, drag her loose pajama bottoms from her body and bury himself in her heat.

But he wouldn't.

He'd learned a long time ago that one-night stands left him feeling unsatisfied, so he'd made a practice of not engaging in them. Besides, he wanted more from Maggie Copeland than just sex, no matter how incredible it promised to be. He wanted to imprint himself on her; to ensure she wouldn't forget him after one night. When he made love to her, he wanted it to mean something.

"I'm not sure that's a good idea," he said carefully.

For a moment, Maggie stared blankly at him, and then hot color washed into her face. She looked so mortified that Jack wanted to haul her into his arms and kiss away her confusion.

"Oh, my God," she said, covering her face with her hands. "I'm sorry. It's just that I thought—" Dropping her hands, she gave him a helpless look. "I misunderstood."

With a rueful smile, Jack stepped closer until he was crowding her against the open door. He slid a hand along her jaw, caressing the smooth skin of her cheek with his thumb. "There's no misunderstanding, Maggie. I'd love to take you to bed, I really would."

She searched his face, bewildered. "Then why don't you?"

"Because you'd hate yourself tomorrow and worse, you'd hate me."

"No, I—"

He put his thumb over her mouth, silencing her. "It's okay. I fully intend to sleep with you, Maggie Copeland." He smiled as her eyes widened. "Just not tonight."

"Oh." She was silent for a moment, and then her gaze dropped to his mouth. "Well then. How about a good-night kiss?"

With a small groan of defeat, Jack pulled her toward him and covered her mouth with his own. She tasted just as he remembered, like wild honey and the tang of the sea. She made a soft sound of approval and leaned into him, deepening the kiss. Jack welcomed the silken intrusion of her tongue, and the moist fusing of their lips caused lust to jackknife through his gut. He slid one hand to the small of her back and drew her closer so that she couldn't mistake his growing arousal, or her effect on him.

"God, you taste good," he muttered against her mouth.

She pulled back and he could see the heat in her eyes. "Are you sure I can't change your mind?"

Jack gave a low laugh. "Oh, sweetheart, you are making it so damned hard for me to do the right thing here."

He knew if he didn't leave now, he might not leave at all, so he reluctantly set her away from him. He told himself he was making the right decision; he needed to be at the airfield early the following morning, and he needed to be rested and clearheaded.

"Okay." Maggie's skin was flushed, and in the indistinct light, her eyes were smoky with desire. "I'll let you off easy this time."

But as Jack walked back to the cottage with his hands thrust into his pockets, he knew she hadn't let him off easy at all. He'd spend most of the night awake and aching, and he'd feel the effects tomorrow. But he knew he'd made the right choice in walking away, even if it felt completely wrong.

MAGGIE PAUSED IN the act of arranging jewelry in a glass display case, and cocked her head, listening. Two jets rocketed overhead, the rumble of their engines causing the windows of the small shop to tremble.

"I swear, those flyboys come a little closer every day," grumbled Carly from the other side of the room. "I didn't think they were allowed to fly over here."

Maggie waited until the sound of the jets faded in the distance, and then stood back to study the collection of necklaces and earrings, artfully arranged on the white silk with bits of sea glass and some polished beach pebbles. "I like the sound," she mused. "I remember lying on the beach as a kid and watching the jets perform maneuvers along the coast. It was like a never-ending air show, every day."

Carly looked up from the counter where she was writing an order and gave Maggie a fond smile. "I seem to remember you spending more time traipsing all over the island with your camera in hand, searching for the perfect picture. But I do recall how you loved the sound of those jets."

Maggie laughed. "I wanted to be a fighter pilot in the worst way. And if I couldn't do that, I wanted to marry a fighter pilot." She sobered instantly. "I was so stupid."

Carly came around from the counter and enfolded Maggie in a sympathetic hug, despite the fact she had to stand on her toes to do so. "You were a lot of things, Maggie Copeland—strong-willed, passionate and stubborn, but you were never stupid."

Ridiculous as it seemed, Maggie found herself tearing up under the other woman's compassion. Carly had been like a second mother to her for as far back as she could remember. She was her own mother's best friend, and had helped to run the family business in downtown Coupeville since it had first opened nearly twenty years earlier.

Now Maggie returned her hug. "Thanks, Carly." She pulled away and swiped self-consciously at her damp eyes. "You'd think that after ten years I'd be over it, right?"

"You *are* over it," Carly said briskly. "But you haven't been back to Whidbey Island in ten years, so it's completely natural that all those old memories would return."

Carly was right. She'd left Whidbey Island ten years

ago in desperation, needing to escape the pain and humiliation of watching the man she loved start a new life with another woman. Maybe Chicago hadn't provided the catharsis she'd been looking for, but at least there hadn't been daily reminders of what she'd lost. Being back on Whidbey Island brought all the memories of Phillip rushing back.

Needing a moment to compose herself, Maggie ducked into the back room of the shop and determinedly began to unpack a box of hand-blown glass mermaids that had arrived earlier that day from a local artist. Closing her eyes, she recalled the day she'd discovered Phillip's betrayal. Maybe Carly was right and she hadn't been stupid, but she'd certainly been naive.

She'd met Phillip Woodman the summer after she'd graduated from high school, before she'd left for college. She and a bunch of friends had gone to an air show at Whidbey Naval Air Station, and Maggie had been in heaven as she'd watched the air maneuvers. The show had also provided her with the opportunity to get a close-up look at the jets—and pilot Phillip "Woodie" Woodman. Just twenty-five years old, he'd been the most beautiful man she'd ever seen, with his sun-streaked blond hair and twinkling blue eyes.

Maggie had fallen instantly in love.

They had spent a lot of time together that summer, at least as much as his schedule would allow. He'd explained to her that his job as a navy pilot required him to be gone much of the time, but she'd been unprepared to have him disappear for several weeks at a time to support various missions. But when he was around, he made it clear that he wanted to spend his time with Maggie. She'd been so convinced that he was The One that she'd declined her acceptance to Seattle University in order to stay on Whidbey Island and be closer to Phillip.

Her mother hadn't understood. In fact, she'd been furious and had done everything she could to discourage the relationship and encourage Maggie to complete her education. But there was no reason to think that Phillip would abandon her the way her father had once abandoned her mother. Any fears she might have had were completely allayed when Phillip had proposed marriage during the annual Coupeville arts-and-crafts festival.

She and Phillip had been strolling through the fair admiring the various artists, and had walked out along the enormous pier to the restaurant at the end. He'd bought them both ice cream, and as they'd sat on a bench overlooking the water, he'd asked her to marry him. Maggie could still recall how dizzy she'd been with happiness, unable to believe she was going to become Lieutenant Phillip Woodman's wife. He'd given her a sapphire solitaire because he'd said it matched her eyes.

Three weeks later, when he'd told her he would be leaving for a six-month sea tour aboard the aircraft carrier *USS Abraham Lincoln,* Maggie had wanted to get married before he left. But Phillip had balked, saying he didn't want to rush anything, and that she deserved a big wedding with all the bells and whistles. They would get married as soon as he returned.

So Maggie had bid him farewell, and had thrown herself into the wedding preparations. She and her mother had purchased a gown, chosen the bridesmaids, selected a caterer and a band and ordered the invitations. And then the unthinkable happened.

Maggie would never forget the day she had run into a high school girlfriend in Oak Harbor, who had told her she'd run into Phillip the week before. Maggie hadn't believed her—she hadn't *wanted* to believe her. Because that would mean that he'd either lied to her about the length of his deployment, or he'd returned three months early, but didn't miss her enough to let her know. Either option was almost too horrible for her to bear.

She'd left voice messages for him, asking him to return her calls, but two days passed without a word. Finally, unable to stand it, Maggie had driven over to the air base. Without a military ID, she hadn't been allowed access. She'd stood outside the visitor's center, feeling frustrated and panicky, when a car had drove up to the guard house and she'd recognized the driver as one of Phillip's friends and fellow pilots. She'd approached him and asked if he knew anything about Phillip's return, but the man had only looked uncomfortable, before telling her that Phillip had never deployed.

Maggie had been stunned.

Now she shook off the disturbing memories and focused instead on attaching price tags to the glass mermaids. She hadn't wanted to return to Whidbey Island because she'd known it would open the floodgates to all those old, painful memories, but she also knew that she couldn't hide from them forever.

Like it or not, they were a part of her, and the best she could hope for was that she'd learned something from the experience—like not to get involved with a guy in uniform, no matter how hot he might be.

She gave a soft huff of self-deprecating laughter. She'd never learn. She'd been home for less than four days and already she'd propositioned an airman whom she barely knew. Remembering his promise that he would sleep with her, Maggie smiled and picked up several of the mermaids, looping their strings over her fingers as she carried them into the main part of the shop.

"I thought these would look great hanging in the window," she said to Carly, showing her the ornaments.

"They're lovely," Carly said, "and they'll sell like hotcakes."

"That's what I thought, too." Maggie began to hang the mermaids in the front windows, alongside several blown-glass starfish and seahorses. While the shop primarily showcased the sea-glass jewelry collections that Eric and Danielle created, it also featured the work of several local glass blowers.

"What are you going to sell at the festival?" Carly asked.

Maggie's mother was a talented jeweler, and when both Eric and Maggie had demonstrated some artistic skill of their own, she had encouraged them to pursue fine arts as a career. Like their mother, Eric specialized in creating handcrafted, sea-glass jewelry. His wife, Danielle, had also started a line of cocktail glasses and utensils adorned with sea glass.

Maggie had wanted to illustrate children's books, until she'd discovered photography in her early teens. Her mother had installed a darkroom for her in the former pantry of their house, and Maggie had quickly learned how to use special developing techniques to enhance her photos.

She shrugged. "I hadn't planned on selling anything. I didn't bring any of my photos with me from Chicago."

"The festival isn't for another week," Carly said. "You could have something ready before then. I remember you once did a whole series of note cards that were very popular."

Maggie gave her a tolerant look. "As I recall, the only

ones who bought those cards were you, my mother and her friends."

Carly laughed. "I still have several sets of those cards, and I still send them out to family and friends. But it would be nice if you had something to put in the show. You're very talented, Maggie."

A young couple entered the shop, causing the small bells over the door to tinkle, effectively putting a stop to their conversation. But as the afternoon passed, Maggie wondered if she might actually be able to put something together in time for the festival. She thought about the photos she'd taken of the orca whale. She hadn't had time to develop the film, and now she wondered how the pictures had come out. She hadn't done any wild-life photography since she was a teenager, but found she was excited about developing the film and seeing the results.

Although Maggie was trained in digital photography and while most of her clients preferred that, her preference was for the 35mm camera, and she used film for her own personal work. But it had been years since she'd used the darkroom in her mother's house. She'd probably need to restock the chemicals and supplies and purchase some new photo stock. She hadn't thought she'd be interested in showing anything at the art festival, but now that the idea had been planted, she found it quickly taking root. She had her camera, and she'd brought her assortment of lenses and filters, along with a hefty supply of film. The prospect of working in the darkroom, where she'd spent so many hours as a teenager, appealed to her.

The sun was beginning to set, and she and Carly were just closing up the shop when the bells over the door jangled. Maggie automatically looked up to greet the customer and tell them she was getting ready to close, when the words died on her lips. Jack Callahan stood in the doorway, one hand still on the latch as he pulled his hat off with his free hand.

Maggie drank him in, aware that her heart was popping rapidly against her chest. He wore the one-piece jumpsuit of a navy pilot, and she'd never seen anyone look as drop-dead gorgeous in it as he did.

Not even Phillip.

Talk about walking sex in a flight suit! The coveralls emphasized the broad thrust of his shoulders and the trimness of his waist and hips. Unbidden, Maggie imagined herself unzipping the suit. In her fantasy, he'd be naked underneath, and she would slide her hands inside the fabric to caress him.

Leaning weakly against the nearby counter, she lifted her heavy ponytail away from her neck. Was it her imagination, or had the temperature in the small store suddenly spiked?

"Hey," he said, when she didn't say anything. "I noticed you walked into town this morning, so I thought I'd offer you a lift back to the house. If you're interested, that is."

Maggie was interested in more than just a ride, but she kept her thoughts to herself. She glanced at Carly, who looked as awestruck by the sight of him as she probably did.

"Well—" she began, only to be interrupted by Carly.

"She could use a ride. She worked hard today, and if you ask me, it looks as if it might rain."

Both Maggie and Jack turned to look through the window at the brilliant sunset, and Maggie thought she saw Jack hide a smile.

"Thank you," she said quickly, not wanting to hear

what Carly might say next. "Let me just collect my things from the back room."

As she grabbed her backpack and sweater from where she had left them in the stockroom, she heard the low rumble of Jack's voice as he spoke to Carly, and her answering laugh. She sounded like a smitten schoolgirl.

"All set?" Jack asked, as she reentered the shop.

Maggie nodded. "Yes. Carly, are you okay to lock up?"

Carly gave her a beatific smile. "I've been doing it for almost twenty years, hon, so I think I can manage. You go ahead, and I'll see you tomorrow."

"Okay, then. Good night."

She followed Jack along the sidewalk to where he had parked his vehicle, and murmured her thanks as he opened the passenger door and helped her in. She watched as he walked around the front and then climbed into the driver's seat.

"So you're a pilot." It was a statement, not a question, and his hand paused in the act of turning the key in the ignition.

He slanted her a quizzical look. "I am. How did you know?"

She gestured to his shoulder, where an insignia patch bore the name of his squadron. "Well, that for starters. And the fact that you're wearing a flight suit." She peered at his name tag. *Jack Callahan.* Beneath his name was the word *Mick.* "That's your call sign? Mick?"

Jack grinned ruefully. "Not very original, I know."

"What does it mean?"

He gave her a tolerant look. "Mick as in Irish. The guys in my squadron call me McCallahan, hence the call sign."

"Ah. So what do you fly? Growlers or Prowlers?"

"You know something about aircraft?"

"When you grow up on Whidbey Island, it's kind of impossible not to know about the aircraft that are flying overhead," she said drily.

"Growlers. I fly Growlers." Releasing the key, he sat back in the seat and considered her for a moment. "Are you okay? You look a little pale."

Maggie was laughing softly, and she couldn't seem to stop. The universe certainly had a quirky sense of humor. He wasn't just a guy who worked at the air base. He wasn't just an airman. He was a *pilot*. What were the chances that she'd find herself attracted to another pilot? Why couldn't he have been a regular, run-of-the-mill sailor, or a maintenance officer? She'd heard that most women had a type, and it seemed hers was the sexy flyboy.

"I'm fine," she said, controlling her mirth. She drew in a fortifying breath and wiped her eyes. "Don't mind me."

He quirked an eyebrow at her. "You're sure? When did you last eat?"

"This morning." She hesitated as a thought occurred to her. "Do you like pasta?"

Jack gave her a suspicious look. "Is this a trick question?"

Maggie laughed softly. "No. But I make a pretty mean shrimp Alfredo. If you're interested…"

"I am," he said quickly, and grinned. "I most definitely am."

5

MAGGIE WASN'T SURE what had prompted her to extend a dinner invitation to Jack, but as she prepared for the evening, she found herself as nervous as a teenager on her first date. She'd set a table for them on the wide, covered verandah, with a view of the water through the trees. Strains of music drifted toward her from inside the kitchen. At some point, her brother—or maybe Danielle—had strung minilights along the ceiling of the porch, and now they twinkled softly in the darkness.

Surveying the scene through critical eyes, she hoped she hadn't overdone the romantic atmosphere. She didn't deny that she found Jack Callahan attractive, and she may even have indulged in an erotic daydream or two about him, but she wasn't sure she could handle another rejection tonight.

She'd been ready to jump him last night, but after a long day of weighing the pros and cons of getting involved with him, she was no longer sure it was a great idea. She'd only be around for three weeks. She had absolutely no plans to stay longer than that, and long-distance relationships weren't her forte. So where did that leave them?

She'd never had a relationship based purely on physical attraction; she'd always been emotionally invested in whomever she'd slept with. Not that there had been a lot of men in her life, but you didn't get to be twenty-eight years old without having some history. But she hadn't had a serious guy in her life for almost a year, and she'd be the first to admit that her hormones were getting a little restless.

What if he indicated he wanted to spend the night with her? What would she say? Could she sleep with him and still leave in three weeks? Could she let him into her bed without letting him into her heart? She didn't know.

A light knock startled her, and she turned to see Jack standing at the far end of the verandah, his hand raised against one of the wooden pillars. Maggie swallowed hard. He looked delicious in a pair of worn, faded jeans and a white, button-down shirt that was rolled up over his forearms. Maggie found him incredibly sexy.

"Am I on time?" he asked with a smile as he walked toward her.

Maggie nodded, devouring him with her eyes. "Yes, you're right on time."

"Good." He extended a bottle of wine toward her. "I was told this would go well with pasta and seafood."

She took the bottle from him and examined the label. "Very nice. Thank you. Come into the kitchen and help me finish up?"

"You bet." He opened the screen door and indicated she should precede him into the house. "Something smells great."

"The pasta should be just about ready, and the Alfredo sauce and shrimp are done. I just need to finish the salad, and then we can eat."

"Sounds good," he said, setting the wine down on the counter. "How about I pour us each a glass of wine?"

"Mmm, that sounds great."

She handed Jack a corkscrew and watched as he effortlessly uncorked the bottle and poured them each a glass. Their fingers brushed as he handed her the wine and a thrill of awareness shot through Maggie.

"Here's to…new friendships."

Maggie gave him a quick smile. "To new friendships."

They touched glasses and Maggie watched as he took a swallow of wine, his eyes never leaving hers.

"Try it," he said, lowering his glass.

Maggie took a sip. "It's delicious."

"You look amazing, by the way."

His gaze drifted over her, and Maggie found herself blushing beneath his masculine regard. She hadn't brought any clothing with her that was suitable for a date, so she had raided Danielle's closet. She'd finally settled on a sleeveless dress in a soft turquoise, patterned with cream flowers. She was taller than Danielle, and the dress was tighter across the bust than she would have liked, but the design was feminine and flattering.

"Thanks," she murmured. "You look pretty good yourself."

He grinned, and setting his wine down on the counter, turned his attention to the bowl of vegetables. "Can I help with the salad?"

Maggie nodded, and as Jack prepared the salad, she arranged two plates of pasta with shrimp Alfredo sauce, but every cell in her body was acutely aware of the man standing next to her. The kitchen was large, with an enormous center island and high ceilings, yet he made it seem small with his presence.

"I'm declaring the meal ready," she said, turning to him.

Jack indicated the salad with a grin. "Perfect timing, because I'm declaring the salad ready, too."

Without waiting, he tucked the wine bottle beneath one arm, and then scooped up the salad and both of their wineglasses. "Can you manage the plates?"

Maggie nodded. "Absolutely."

She followed him onto the porch and waited while he set down the salad and wine, and then took both plates from her hands and placed them on the table.

"Allow me," he said, and pulled her chair back for her.

When they were both seated, Maggie busied herself with serving the salad, aware of him watching her. "I'm glad you were able to come over tonight."

"That makes two of us," he replied, and picked up his fork. "But I'm curious—why did you invite me for dinner?"

Maggie shrugged, but couldn't quite meet his gaze. How would he react if she told him that dinner seemed an appropriate lead-in to inviting him to spend the night? "You're new to the area," she said, instead, "and I know it's what my brother and his wife would have done."

"Ah," he said, with meaning. "So you only invited me out of a sense of duty."

Maggie's gaze flew to his. "What? No! Of course not. I *wanted* to invite you."

"I'm teasing you, Maggie," he said, and reached across the table to cover her hand with his. "If you hadn't invited me over, I was going to ask you to go to dinner with me somewhere."

Maggie blinked. "You were?"

He grinned. "Yeah. There's a little Italian place in Oak Harbor that's supposed to be good. But I think this is much, much better."

He didn't release her hand, and Maggie gathered the courage to curl her fingers around his. "I agree. This is better."

Giving her hand a light squeeze, Jack released her and began to dig into his meal with such enthusiasm that Maggie had to hide a smile. Jack paused midbite and looked at her, and then gave her a rueful grin as he set down his fork.

"Sorry," he said, sounding anything but regretful. "I can't remember the last time I had something this delicious. I guess I got carried away."

"You're kidding, right? I'm not exactly known for my culinary skills."

"Trust me, this is fantastic."

Picking up her fork, Maggie took a bite of the pasta and shrimp.

"Mmm," she agreed. "Not bad at all. The recipe is my mom's, but it always helps to have fresh seafood literally at your doorstep."

Jack tore off a chunk of bread from the crusty loaf that Maggie had placed in a basket on the table, and took a bite. "Well, my compliments to both you and your mother. Does she live nearby?"

"No. She lives in California with her boyfriend."

"Ah." Jack gave her an understanding look. "My parents split when I was a kid, so I know how tough it can be, especially when they find a new significant other. What about your dad? Is he on Whidbey Island?"

Maggie had known that it would only be a matter of time before he learned the truth of her upbringing; she just hadn't expected it to be so soon. She swirled the wine in her glass and admired the play of candlelight through the amber liquid.

"I never knew my father," she finally said, and took a hefty swallow of her wine.

Jack was silent for a moment. "I'm sorry. I didn't mean to upset you."

"No, you didn't." She waved a hand in dismissal. "Like I said, I never knew him. He pretty much abandoned my mother when he found out she was pregnant with me and my brother."

"Were they married?"

Maggie gave him a bright smile. "No. He was an airman, and my mother was barely nineteen. She was young and foolish, and believed him when he said he would marry her."

"He *left* her?" Jack's voice reflected his astonishment and anger. "Did he at least provide financial support for the three of you?"

"At first, I think he did. But then he got out of the military and from what I understand, he pretty much vanished."

Jack snorted. "Vanished, my ass. He took a job somewhere that paid cash. Kind of hard to garnish his wages when he's getting paid under the table." Leaning back in his chair, he scrubbed a hand over his face. "Christ, I'm sorry, Maggie. No wonder you're a little gun-shy."

Maggie wanted to hug him, he was so sincere in his outrage. Was he right about her being gun-shy? Oh, yeah, but not for the reasons he believed. Which was why she'd call all the shots in whatever developed between them. If she went into this thing with her eyes wide open and her emotions under strict control, she'd be okay—whatever happened. Now she looked at Jack and smiled.

"Well, you know what they say...fool me once, shame on you—fool me twice, shame on me."

To her surprise, Jack reached across the table and caught her hand, pressing her fingers between the warm strength of his own.

"I'm not going to hurt you, Maggie."

His voice was so low and compelling that for an instant, Maggie found herself believing him, before she determinedly pulled her hand away and pushed it down onto her lap.

JACK DIDN'T KNOW what to make of Maggie Copeland. She was a mass of contradictions. He hadn't been kidding when he said she looked amazing, but despite the fact she'd obviously dressed up for him, her wary manner told him to tread softly. He tried, but failed, to keep from staring at her. The candlelight made her skin more luminous, and the neckline of her dress teased him with tantalizing glimpses of her breasts where the fabric gaped away a bit. Whereas she'd appeared outwardly tough and capable the day he'd found her performing plumbing work on his kitchen sink, even swearing like a sailor, tonight she seemed impossibly feminine and fragile. He wanted to forego dinner and devour her instead.

He felt honored that she'd trusted him enough to share the details of her birth with him, although the facts seriously pissed him off. There was a part of him that wanted to hunt down her deadbeat father and beat the crap out of him for the damage he'd done to his daughter. He'd known guys in the service who'd knocked up their girlfriends, but he didn't know any who had completely washed their hands of their parental responsibilities, even if they'd chosen not to marry the mother. And if they had tried to shirk their duties in that regard, the military usually ensured they provided at least the minimum financial support. He couldn't imagine what kind of man would abandon a girl who was pregnant with his child, or in the case of Maggie's mother, his children. At least now he understood why Maggie was so reticent about military men. His own father had been career air force. Although his parents had remained married for most of his childhood, his father had been gone more than he'd been home. Had he and his mother felt abandoned? Oh, yeah.

Sensing her unease with the direction of the conversation, he concentrated on his food and strove for a casual tone. "My parents got divorced when I was ten. I wanted to live with my dad, but he was in the air force and moved around a lot, so I mostly lived with my mom."

"In Florida?"

"No, that was just where my last assignment was. I was born and raised in Boulder, Colorado."

"Really?" Her voice registered surprise. "I pictured you on a surfboard somewhere."

Jack liked the fact that she'd been picturing him anywhere, although his preference would be for her to picture him in her bed, doing hedonistic things to her.

"I've done some surfing," he acknowledged, "but rock climbing is more my speed."

Maggie laughed softly. "Of course it is. I remember the night we met, when I was stuck on that rock and you asked me if I was experienced with bouldering. Is that the same as rock climbing?"

"Similar, but it's done without any climbing equipment."

"That sounds dangerous."

"Like anything, you have to use common sense. Bouldering is done with a crash pad on the ground, which provides some cushion if you do fall. And most bouldering is done on rocks that are less than forty feet high. Any higher than that, and you risk serious injury if you do fall."

Maggie made a sound that was half laugh and half groan. "Forty feet? You must have thought I was so pathetic the night I was stuck on that baby rock. How high was that? Ten feet?"

"More like fifteen, but still too high for you to jump down from. And I didn't think you were pathetic. I'm just glad I was there."

He recalled those moments when he'd stood at the far end of the rocky beach, and she had emerged from the trailhead with her camera slung over her body. She'd been so intent on the orca that she hadn't even noticed him.

But he had noticed her.

She'd scrambled to the top of the boulder without any problem, and he'd enjoyed watching her work, snapping pictures in quick succession. She'd been so engrossed in what she'd been doing that she hadn't been aware of her surroundings. But as the few other tourists began drifting away from the beach and making their way back to the parking lot, he'd stayed behind. He'd been reluctant to leave her alone on the dark shoreline, and when she'd had trouble negotiating her way down from the boulder, he'd been glad that he'd stayed.

"I'm glad, too," she murmured softly.

As she gazed at him, Jack saw the awareness in her

eyes. If he'd had any doubts about her attraction to him, they were completely dispelled by that one look, and Jack felt his body tighten in anticipation. As if realizing how much she'd revealed, she tried to hide her reaction by hastily downing her entire glass of wine.

"Easy," he said with a soft laugh. Reaching across the table, he took the empty wineglass from her and set it aside. "It's deceptively strong."

"I see," she said in mock indignation as she swiped a finger over her mouth. "So now you're trying to get me drunk?"

"Oh, no, sweetheart," he said, letting his voice drop to a seductive drawl. "I prefer my women coherent and responsive."

For a moment she just stared at him, and then her mouth opened on a soft "oh" of realization. She swallowed once, and then looked helplessly at her nearly untouched plate, before directing her gaze back at him. "Do you want dessert?"

He wanted *her*. Badly. Right now, she looked like the sweetest thing on the menu.

"Sure. Why not?" He indicated her plate. "Are you finished? You've barely touched your meal."

She had a lock of hair that refused to stay confined in her ponytail, and instead bounced enticingly against the curve of her cheek. Now she tucked it behind her ear in a self-conscious gesture.

"I'm not hungry."

But when she looked at him, her gaze was so greedy that for just an instant, Jack found himself unable to breathe. She broke the spell by springing to her feet and snatching her own plate from the table.

"I'll get the dishes," she said quickly, and before he

could protest, she filled her arms with plates and bowls and hurried into the kitchen.

Jack took a moment to compose himself and then followed her at slower pace, carrying the bottle of wine and their glasses. From the refrigerator, Maggie had pulled out two fluted glass dishes filled with what looked like chocolate pudding, and was spraying whipped cream onto them in a haphazard manner that betrayed her agitation. She was getting more on herself and the counter than she did on the dessert.

Placing the wine and the glasses on a nearby surface, he moved until he stood directly behind her. He could smell the fragrance of her hair and skin, see the tiny pulse that beat frantically at the side of her neck and hear her shallow breathing.

"Maggie."

She turned her head, but didn't meet his eyes. "I came back to Whidbey Island expecting a lot of things," she confessed softly. Turning fully around, she leaned against the counter and looked at him. "But I never expected you."

Jack raised a hand and gently wound the loose tendril of hair around his finger before tucking it behind her ear. He used his thumb to wipe away several flecks of whipped cream from her cheek. "Yeah, well, I wasn't expecting you, either."

She searched his eyes for a long moment, and then exhaled on a shaky breath. "I know this is crazy, but I really want—"

Leaning forward, Jack covered her mouth with his.

6

THIS WAS WHAT she'd been craving. This man.

Kissing her. Touching her.

Making her feel things that she hadn't felt in over ten years.

Maggie leaned into him, giving herself up to his kiss. His mouth moved over hers, warm and firm, and when she felt the first, hesitant touch of his tongue, she deepened the kiss. Immediately, he cupped her jaw in his big hands and angled her face for better access, fusing his mouth to hers. The sheer sensuality of the contact made her go weak, and she clutched mindlessly at his shirt as he explored her mouth. His tongue slid sensuously against hers, and she felt an answering rush of desire at her center. Beneath the soft cotton, his body was firm and hot, and Maggie knew exactly where she wanted all that heat and strength.

Breaking the kiss, she leaned back in his arms. A flush of arousal rode high on his cheekbones, and his expression was taut. Catching her lower lip between her teeth, Maggie tentatively smoothed a hand over his chest, before unfastening the top button of his shirt.

When he didn't object, she moved to the next button, spreading the soft fabric and exposing his skin. Leaning forward, she pressed a soft, moist kiss just below his collarbone. He sucked in a breath, and one big hand moved to the back of her head to massage the nape of her neck. Emboldened, Maggie tasted him, touching her tongue to his heated skin and tracing a delicate circle over the shallow groove between his pecs. Jack made a hissing sound of pleasure, and beneath her fingers, she could feel the heavy thump of his heart.

"You taste good," she murmured against his skin.

Wrapping her ponytail around his fist, Jack gently tugged her head back so that her face was tilted upward. "You're driving me nuts," he rasped.

His husky admission thrilled Maggie. She'd never been the kind of woman who deliberately set out to entice men, or lead them on. In fact, those who knew her well would probably say she went out of her way to avoid attracting attention from the opposite sex. She didn't consider herself unattractive, but she definitely wasn't the type who garnered wolf whistles or even second looks when she went out.

She rarely wore makeup, and since her hair pretty much defied any style, she found it easier to just pull it back in a clip or a ponytail. She preferred jeans to dresses, and she had a bad habit of swearing that she knew could be disconcerting. The fact that this man found her attractive blew her mind. She didn't even care what his motives might be; she no longer believed in fairy tales, and had no illusions that his interest in her extended beyond one or two interludes of shared pleasure. Right now, that sounded perfect to her. She neither wanted nor needed an emotional entanglement, and with her mom and brother away, nobody even needed to know that she had hooked up with the tenant. She felt certain he wouldn't say anything.

"I want to drive you nuts," she said, spreading his shirt open even more and punctuating her words with another damp kiss, this time directly above his nipple. She glanced up at him as she swirled her tongue over the small bud. "I want to push you right over the edge."

JACK DRAGGED AIR into his lungs and tried to control his rampant lust. Her words, combined with the soft, hot slide of her tongue against his skin, were an aphrodisiac he couldn't resist. She said she wanted to push him over the edge, but he was already there, just barely hanging on.

He'd been surprised by the invitation to have dinner with her, but even knowing she was attracted to him, he hadn't planned on doing anything about it, at least not tonight. He wanted to ensure she had at least a little bit of emotional investment in their relationship before they slept together. Now he found himself reassessing his strategy.

Maggie leaned back in his arms and looked up at him. Her pupils were dilated, making her dark blue eyes appear almost black, and her pale cheeks were slightly flushed. When his gaze dropped to her mouth, she moistened her lips, sending a jolt of lust straight to his groin. Her mouth was lush and pink, and his imagination ran rampant with erotic images. Her breath came in warm pants against his neck, and her breasts rose and fell in an agitated fashion. He wanted to devour her. He wanted to peel the dress away from her body, lift her onto the nearby table and thrust himself into her. He wanted to hear her cry out in pleasure, watch her expression as she reached her orgasm and then start all over again.

"Sweetheart," he growled softly, "I'm so close to the edge now that in another second I'll be free-falling." He bent his head to her exposed throat and kissed the spot where her pulse beat, sucking gently on her soft flesh before soothing the area with his tongue. She made a small noise, half groan and half sigh, and tipped her head to give him better access.

"You taste good, too," he muttered against her skin, before he dragged his mouth along her jaw and captured her lips again. This time, he kissed her hard and deep, entwining his tongue with hers. Her arms wound around his neck and she pressed closer, opening herself to him.

Jack didn't think she was even aware of how she rubbed herself sensuously against him, like a small cat, but he was all too mindful, and he couldn't prevent his body's immediate response. He had a boner for her, big-time, and in another second, she'd be aware of it, too.

He slid his arms around her, stroking his hands down her back to her rear. The woman definitely had curves in all the right places, and he ached to explore every one of them. He could have her right now, he knew. The soft, needy sounds she made in her throat were a huge turn-on, but he needed to slow this down or he'd end up taking her right here in the kitchen. Breaking the kiss, he bent his forehead to hers. They were both breathing heavily, and her fingers caressed the nape of his neck.

"How about that dessert?" His voice was roughened with desire, but he was gratified when she gave a soft giggle.

"I thought that *was* dessert."

"That was just the appetizer," he assured her, and reluctantly released her.

She drew in a deep breath and swayed slightly before she grasped the edge of the counter for support. When she looked at him, he noted with satisfaction that her eyes were still a little hazy with pleasure. He'd left a mark at the base of her throat, no more than a reddened patch where he'd sucked on her soft skin, but he felt a deep satisfaction in that, as well.

Reaching out, she scooped up a finger of whipped cream and offered it to him. Jack's libido leaped at the implicit promise in her eyes, and he brought her hand to his mouth and sucked the cream from her finger. Her lips parted in a soft "oh" of pleasure, and he knew she'd felt it all the way to her toes.

"My turn," he said, and dipped his thumb into the chocolate pudding. But when she drew his finger into her mouth and sucked on it, lust jackknifed through his gut and he nearly groaned aloud at the erotic sensation. Her tongue was hot and slick, and he could almost feel the suction on his dick.

When she finally released his finger, Jack's imagination was running wild with images of her mouth wrapped around other parts of his anatomy.

"If I suggest moving this somewhere more…comfortable," she ventured carefully, "are you going to get all honorable on me and insist on leaving?"

"Do you want me to stay?"

In answer, she slid her arms around his neck and moved closer, until her breasts were all but flattened against his chest. "I do. I want you to stay the night."

Her voice wavered the slightest bit, and Jack knew how much it had cost her to admit that to him. Her body fit perfectly against his own, and as his hands moved over her back to the curve of her ass, he knew he wouldn't refuse her. He couldn't.

"Yeah," he rasped. "I'll stay."

With her arms around his neck, Jack bent and slid an arm beneath her knees, lifting her high against his chest before she had a chance to protest. She gasped and clutched him tighter, and Jack was reminded of the night when they had first met, when he'd pulled her down off the boulder.

"Where are we going?" he asked, turning toward the staircase that led to the second floor.

"Upstairs, second door on the left."

Jack practically sprinted up the stairs, and shouldered his way into the room she'd indicated. Inside, he had a vague impression of a canopy bed, and made a beeline for it, depositing Maggie on the mattress, before stretching out beside her. Almost immediately, he rose up on his elbow, and reached beneath him to pull out a stuffed animal.

"What is this?" he asked, studying it in the dark.

"Sorry," Maggie said, and taking the toy from him, she chucked it across the room. "Now come here."

Her hands went to his shoulders, and as Jack moved toward her, something hard dug into his hip. Pulling away, he sat up and withdrew a doll from beneath his body. "Okay, what's this?"

Maggie groaned, and took the doll from him and dropped it onto the floor beside the bed. "This is the room I used as a kid," she said ruefully. "I guess it could use some updating."

Stretching his arm out, Jack flipped on the bedside lamp and looked around the room, appalled. There was pink everywhere. Even the ruffled canopy over their heads was pink, matched by the bedspread and flowered carpet. There were stuffed animals and dolls on nearly every surface, and the walls were plastered with posters of young male pop stars from at least a decade earlier. The room was more suited to a ten-year-old child than a twenty-something woman.

Climbing off the bed, Jack grabbed Maggie by the hands and pulled her to her feet. "No offense, sweetheart, but there's no way I can make love to you in this room. I'm not sure I could even take my shirt off in this room without feeling like a pervert."

"Okay, I understand," Maggie said quickly. "This isn't the only bedroom. We can use one of the others."

Jack gave a snort of laughter. "Like your brother's room? Thanks, but no thanks." Heading for the door, he tugged Maggie along in his wake. "C'mon."

"Where are we going?"

He cast her one meaningful look over his shoulder. "To my room."

Her eyes widened in surprise for an instant, before she gave him a smile filled with anticipation. "Lead on."

As they stepped outside, Jack noticed that the temperature had dropped, and the sun had completely vanished. The path to the cottage was cast in deep shadows, and he hadn't thought to leave a light on in the small house. He glanced down at Maggie, taking in her bare arms and high-heeled sandals. The path was uneven, and it wouldn't take much for her to stumble.

"Here, let me help you," he said, and swept her into his arms once more.

Maggie laughed, a low, sexy sound that sent Jack's blood surging through his veins. "This is getting to be a habit with you," she teased.

"I hope so," he said, pressing a kiss to her neck. Inside the cottage, he didn't pause, but strode through the dark living room to the bedroom, which overlooked the water. Pale moonlight spilled in through the French doors that opened onto the deck, casting the room in silvery shadows. He set Maggie on her feet next to the bed. She was shivering, so he grabbed a soft, woolen throw from the foot of the bed, and wrapped it around her shoulders.

"You're cold."

In answer, she stepped closer to him and slid her arms around his waist. "You can warm me."

Jack's pulse kicked up a notch. In the indistinct light, her face was a pale oval, her eyes enormous and dark. Reaching out, he tugged the elastic from her ponytail and threaded his fingers through her hair, loosening it around her face.

"I like your hair," he murmured. "You should wear it down all the time."

Maggie gave a self-conscious laugh. "It pretty much refuses to stay put, so it's more practical to just pull it back."

"I prefer it like this."

"I think that makes you the first." With a small shrug, she let the blanket fall from her shoulders to pool on the floor around her feet. "I'm not cold anymore."

Jack slid his hands to her shoulders, and then down her bare arms. Her skin still felt cool beneath his fingers. Despite her claim of not being chilled, she shivered beneath his touch.

"Come here," he said, and gathered her close, sliding his hands through her hair to cradle her head and tip her face up for his kiss. Her lips were warm, and as he deepened the kiss, she made a small sound of approval. Her mouth was hot and slick, and if he thought he'd be the one doing the kissing, he was wrong.

Without breaking the kiss, Maggie turned him until the back of his legs bumped against the edge of the bed.

When she gave him a slight push, he complied and sat down on the edge of the mattress. Maggie broke away, her breathing fast and shallow, and Jack watched as she hitched her dress up over her thighs and straddled his legs, looping her arms around his neck and planting moist kisses along his jaw.

"This is where I want you," she whispered into his ear, and then caught his earlobe between her teeth, before soothing the sensitive area with a soft lick of her tongue.

Jack groaned. The weight of her on his thighs was an exquisite torture, and it took all his restraint not to turn her onto her back and fit himself into the soft cradle of her hips. Instead, he let her take the lead. She captured his mouth, fusing her lips over his and stroking her tongue against his. She squirmed on his lap, and Jack cupped her rear, squeezing her pliant flesh and encouraging her to move closer. He ached to slide his hands beneath the hem of her dress and explore her more fully. He had a raging hard-on, and the restriction of his jeans was making it damned uncomfortable to sit upright.

As if sensing this, Maggie pushed against his shoulders, and he obediently lay back on the bed, dragging her down with him until she was sprawled, half-kneeling, over him. He thrust his hands into the thick waves of her hair, reveling in the cool, silken texture. He kissed her hard, tangling his tongue with hers, gratified when she settled over his hips and began moving against him.

He dragged his mouth from hers and sucked in a lungful of air, desperate to regain some equilibrium. Unfazed, Maggie stroked her lips along his throat, alternately biting and licking his flesh, even as her hands worked the remaining buttons on his shirt. She dragged the shirttail free from his jeans and pushed the shirt wide open, exposing him to her gaze. Rocking back on his hips, her hands on his taut stomach, she drank him in.

"Holy crap," she breathed, and stroked a single finger along the groove that bisected his chest and abdomen. "It's like you're wearing one of those molded chest plates, with the sculpted muscles."

Capturing her hand, Jack pressed it against his skin, directly over his heart. "This is me, baby. I'm the real deal."

Her eyes flew to his, uncertain, but Jack didn't so much as crack a smile. He was dead serious. He'd been so determined to take this slow, but time was working against him. That, and Maggie's unexpected sensuality. He hadn't been prepared for her sexy offensive tonight, and there was no way he could resist her. But the last thing he wanted was for her to think he didn't take this relationship—or whatever it was they had—seriously. At thirty-three years old, he was way past one-night stands.

He held his breath as Maggie tentatively explored his body, running her fingertips over the ridges of his taut stomach until they reached the waistband of his jeans.

"I want to see you," she whispered. "All of you."

Jack's cock hardened even more at the implicit promise in her eyes. "Baby," he said, his voice roughened by desire, "you can look, touch and taste to your heart's content."

Even in the dim light, he saw her swallow hard and then moisten her lips before her hands went to the buckle of his belt, slipping it free in a matter of seconds, before unfastening the button beneath. He watched as she drew the zipper down, her eyes riveted on the bulge beneath. When she parted the fabric to expose his boxers, he was so erect that the head of his penis protruded from the waistband.

"Oh," she breathed, and stroked a fingertip over the tip.

Jack clenched his teeth at the exquisite sensation and bit back a groan of pleasure.

"Here," she said, scooting back on his thighs until she could stand up. "Let's take these off."

Needing no further encouragement, Jack sat up and swiftly pulled off his shoes and socks, before shucking both his jeans and boxers, and finally, his shirt. He looked up to see Maggie's gaze fastened on his penis, which was so rigid with arousal that he thought he might actually come apart at the seams. As much as he wanted to reach for her, he'd already decided to let her set the pace, so he lay back across the bed and bent his arms behind his head.

"I'm all yours," he purred, half promise and half challenge.

He couldn't wait to see how she responded.

7

MAGGIE JUST STARED at him. He was supremely male, from his bulging biceps, displayed to full advantage by his pose, to his muscular thighs and big feet, to the stiff erection that lay against his taut stomach. Even the dark tufts of hair beneath his arms were attractive to her. She wanted to sprawl across his body and rub herself all over him.

She liked that he had brought her here, to the cottage. In just the space of a few days, the place felt like his. She hadn't seen much as he'd carried her into the bedroom, but his unmistakable scent lingered on the bedclothes, making her fully aware that she was in his domain. And she liked it.

She took her time looking at him, admiring his contours. There wasn't anything about him that didn't appeal to her, but the biggest turn-on was the expression in his eyes as he watched her. The heat she saw there was so intense that she felt an answering glow deep in her womb, accompanied by a rush of moisture to her center. Finally, she allowed her gaze to drift to his arousal, and her mouth watered at the sight of him. He was large, his skin dark and flushed against the paler skin of his abdomen. Her fingers itched to stroke him.

She could scarcely believe that she was going to have that part of him inside her. Deep inside her. Keeping her eyes on him, she reached beneath her dress and slowly drew her panties off, stepping out of them and kicking them away. She heard Jack's sharply indrawn breath, saw his nostrils flare as if he were trying to catch her scent. She rarely took the initiative during sex, but there was something about Jack—about the way he looked at her—that made her feel almost primal. She wanted to do decadent things to him; she wanted to see him lose control. She wanted to take him, to *mate* with him. He made her feel feminine and powerful, and for tonight, at least, he was all hers.

"Come here," he rasped, and his cock twitched against his stomach as if it, too, beckoned her closer.

Reaching behind her, Maggie found the zipper of the dress and dragged it slowly downward, letting the dress slide from her shoulders and gape away at the front. She was braless. Jack's stare was fastened on her as she boldly let the garment slip downward until it caught on her hips. Her breasts felt full and tight, aching for his touch.

"Do you like what you see?" she asked softly.

"I do," he muttered. "I'm barely holding it together here, babe. Get over here. *Please.*"

Satisfied that she had his full attention, Maggie turned her back to him and then bent forward to ease the fabric over her fanny, deliberately giving him a peep show of what was to come. Slowly, she unfastened the tiny buckles of her sandals and stepped out of them.

He groaned loudly, and then his big hands were on her hips, drawing her backward. He was sitting on the edge of the bed now, and he drew her between his thighs as he pressed his face to the center of her back, kissing her. The sensation of his whisker-roughened face against her skin was a total turn-on, and Maggie covered his hands with her own and pulled them around to her breasts. He obliged her by filling his hands with her. He cupped and kneaded her breasts, and then rolled her nipples between his fingers until they were stiff and aching. Her legs felt weak with pleasure and as if he knew, he drew her down until she was sitting on the edge of the bed between his splayed thighs. He pulled her back until she rested against his chest and he had unobstructed access to all her feminine assets.

His big hands roamed freely, exploring her breasts and rib cage, before dipping lower to caress her stomach and then her thighs. She could feel his erection pressing against her buttocks, hot and hard, and she let her head loll back against his shoulder.

"Your skin is so soft," he muttered against her ear. His hands roamed over her thighs, and then gently spread them apart. "I wonder how you feel…here." He cupped her intimately, and Maggie couldn't prevent her swift hiss of pleasure. He didn't try to explore her further, simply covered her with his hand and applied a gentle pressure as his free hand played with her breast, toying with the nipple. The sensation was so erotic that it took all of Maggie's self-control not to push herself harder against his fingers.

"Oh, yeah," he breathed. "You're like hot silk down here."

Maggie moaned softly. As incredible as it seemed, she could feel the beginnings of an orgasm, and he hadn't even entered her, or touched her clitoris. Turning her face, she found him watching her through glittering eyes.

"Your mouth," she managed to say. "I want your mouth."

She thought she saw a gleam of male satisfaction in his eyes before he covered her lips with his, kissing her hard and deep, sweeping his tongue against hers until she whimpered softly in need and shifted restlessly against his hand.

"This is what you want," he muttered against her mouth, and parted her with his fingers. "Oh, baby, you are so ready."

He slid a finger along the seam of her sex, teasing her until she squirmed and sought his tongue with her own. He stroked one finger over her aching clitoris, and Maggie's hips jerked in response. If he did it again, she'd come, she was that aroused.

Breaking the kiss, Jack surged to his feet in one movement, bringing Maggie with him. Dazed, she didn't resist when he pushed her down onto the bed. "What…?"

"Shh," he soothed, dropping to his knees. "You wanted my mouth, and you're going to have it."

He couldn't mean—oh, God, he did. Raising herself on her elbows, Maggie watched, enthralled, as he pushed her legs open and skated his mouth along the inside of one thigh, alternately biting and kissing her skin. His hands smoothed over her skin until he reached the apex of her legs, caressing the sensitive area around her sex, but not actually touching where she needed him the most.

"Jack," she begged hoarsely.

"Soon, baby," he promised, but his attention was fixed on her. "You are so damned gorgeous down here."

He dragged her toward him, until her rear was at the very edge of the mattress, and then he bent her legs back and draped them over his shoulders. Maggie knew she should feel awkward, but all she could feel was need, so deep and intense that she almost begged him to touch her. She *needed* him to touch her.

But the first touch of his fingers against her aroused flesh was almost more than she could bear, and her hips bucked in response. Jack put an arm across her abdomen to hold her still, and then stroked his fingers over her, swirling her wetness over her throbbing clitoris until her head fell back and she groaned loudly.

"That's it, baby," he crooned, and inserted a finger inside her.

Maggie gasped and pushed against his hand, wanting more of the exquisite sensation. But when he bent forward and put his mouth on her, she couldn't prevent her hoarse cry of pleasure. His tongue was hot and slick, and he swirled it over her swollen flesh while he worked a second finger into her, thrusting them gently as he used his tongue to torture her. Maggie had never experienced anything like it in her entire life.

Lifting her head, she looked down the length of her body to find Jack watching her as he licked at her. The sight of his dark head between her pale thighs was too much. Pressure built and expanded, swirled through her until she knew she wasn't going to last. As if on cue, Jack pulled away, fumbling with something on the floor before he rose to his feet over her. As Maggie watched, he stroked himself twice with his fist, and then rolled a condom over his length.

"I'm not letting you do this without me," he growled. He hooked her legs over his arms, opening her wider, and positioned himself at her entrance. When he looked at her, Maggie saw his expression was taut. "Is this what you want?"

"No, it's what I need," Maggie panted, and reached for him. "*Please,* Jack."

He surged forward, entering her in one smooth, powerful thrust that had Maggie crying out in pleasure. He stretched her, filled her, and completely overwhelmed her with his sheer masculinity. Releasing her legs, he braced his elbows on either side of her.

"Wrap your legs around me." His voice was low and strained, and his arms trembled with effort. Maggie felt an intense satisfaction in knowing he was as affected by this as she was. Obediently, she raised her legs and hooked her ankles around his hips. The movement drove him deeper, and he bent his head to hers with a soft groan. "You are so freaking tight," he muttered.

She hadn't had sex in over a year, so that could be part of it, she supposed, although his size probably had more do with it. She shifted experimentally beneath him, liking the sensation of fullness.

"You feel so good," she breathed, and pressed a kiss against his shoulder.

"You're okay?" he asked.

"Oh, yeah," she assured him, and punctuated her words by lifting her hips.

Jack groaned and turning his face, kissed her long and deep. "I'm so hard for you," he rasped against her lips. "I want this to be good for you, but I'm not sure I can go slow...."

"I don't want you to go slow," Maggie replied, and realized it was the truth. She still throbbed from when he'd used his mouth on her, and she ached for release. "I'm so close...."

As if that was all he needed to hear, Jack began to

move, pulling out and then slowly sinking back into her. Maggie gasped as her sensitized flesh accommodated him, loving the solid weight of him against her body and the ragged sound of his breathing against her neck. She wrapped her arms around him, feeling his muscles bunch beneath her fingers as he began to move faster, pumping into her with strong, sure strokes. For Maggie, nothing else existed except this man and the way he made her feel.

Raising himself on one hand, he watched her face as he pushed into her. His skin gleamed with exertion and his breathing was harsh, but he kept his movements measured.

"Hold on," he growled softly, and grasping her bottom in his big hands, he reared upward until he knelt between her splayed thighs, holding her buttocks flush against his groin. Her legs dangled over his muscular thighs, and Maggie realized this new position gave them both an unobstructed view of where they were joined. Raising her head, she watched as he sank into her, and she clenched her inner muscles around him. The effect was immediate, as he groaned loudly and thrust into her again. The visual impact, combined with the physical sensation, was almost her undoing. He felt like hot steel inside her, and her flesh clamped greedily around him.

"Oh, my God," Maggie breathed, feeling the beginning of a powerful orgasm.

"You're so slick," Jack said hoarsely. "And tight. I don't think I can last."

Releasing her with one hand, he put his fingers in his mouth and then reached down to stroke her. He swirled his thumb over her sensitized clitoris as he thrust into her, and Maggie bucked beneath him.

"Oh, oh," she panted, as the first spasms wracked her body, fisting her around him. "I'm coming...."

"Ah, hell, I'm coming, too," he said through gritted teeth, and pounded into her as wave after wave of release tore through her.

She was still shuddering with small aftershocks when he finally stopped moving, his breathing labored. After several long minutes, he withdrew from her and lay down beside her, dragging her against his chest. Maggie listened to the heavy uneven thumping of his heart, aware that her own was still hammering against her ribs. She wanted to kiss him, but she was so sated and limp that she couldn't even summon enough energy to do that.

Jack's hand traced a lazy pattern along the length of her arm. "Hey," he said quietly, "you okay?"

Maggie smiled and stretched, rubbing her bare foot against his ankle. "I'm not sure. Am I still alive?"

Jack turned his head sharply to look at her. "Did I hurt you?"

She laughed softly and pressed a kiss against his chest. "You almost killed me, but I promise you it was from pleasure."

Jack let out a long breath. "Yeah, well, the same goes here, babe."

Disengaging himself from her, he rolled to the edge of the bed and stood up. "Don't go anywhere," he said. "Let me just clean up, and I'll be right back."

Maggie watched him cross the room. The moonlight cast intriguing shadows over his body, but she could still see the curve of his spine, his firm butt and his long, muscled legs. He disappeared into the bathroom, and she heard the water running. He'd told her not to go anywhere, but that was her cue to leave. More than anything, she wanted to stay, but she didn't want that kind of relationship with Jack. She didn't want to risk falling in love with him. She needed to leave in order to protect herself.

Scooting to the end of the bed, she hunted for her discarded panties, pulling them on quickly before snatching her dress from the floor and stepping into it. She was just feeling for the zipper when Jack returned. He stopped on the threshold and stared at her, and Maggie could sense his surprise.

"What are you doing?"

She glanced at him, and then looked quickly away. He seemed completely unfazed by the fact that he was still buck-naked, but she was all too aware of how mouthwatering he looked. If he touched her again, she'd be toast. She struggled with the zip, catching it in the fabric of the dress in her nervous haste. "I'm getting dressed."

"I can see that. The question is why?"

Maggie bit her lip and yanked hard on the zipper. How could she explain that she needed to leave now, while she could still pretend that it was just about the sex? That if she stayed the night with him, she ran the risk of actually liking him. She didn't want a reason to stay on Whidbey Island, not when she'd spent the past ten years telling herself she was better off living in Chicago.

"I just think it's better if I go back to the house," she said quietly. "Tonight was great, but I don't want to give you the wrong idea."

"Sweetheart," he said, coming to stand in front of her. "It's way too late for that." Putting a finger beneath her chin, he tipped her face up. "Hey, look at me."

Maggie reluctantly did, his nearness and blatant masculinity causing her pulse to start a frantic tattoo inside her chest. But at least when she was looking into his eyes, she could pretend she didn't notice his amazing pecs and cobblestone abs, or his still semi-erect penis. All of that was tempting enough, but what she saw in his eyes was almost her undoing. His expression was both tender and frustrated, as if he struggled to keep his annoyance in check.

"You don't understand," she said, knowing she sounded defensive.

Jack tipped his head down to look directly into her eyes. "Then explain it to me, please, because I'm not getting it. Ten minutes ago, I was inside you. Deep inside you, and you liked it."

"Yes, I liked it," she admitted, letting him see the truth in her eyes.

"Then why are you running away? Stay here tonight. Tomorrow is Sunday, and I don't have to be at the base until noon. We can stay in bed all morning. I'll cook us breakfast."

He made it sound so tempting, and there was a part of Maggie that wanted to give in; to spend the night exploring his body and enjoying what he could do to her. She could handle the incredible sex—and it had been incredible—but staying in his bed for the entire night, and then sharing breakfast with him seemed too intimate. Too cozy. She didn't want to get so emotionally involved with Jack Callahan that she couldn't walk away when the time came for her to return to Chicago.

"Thanks," she finally said, averting her gaze, "but I need to be up early in the morning."

A total fib, but he didn't have to know that.

Jack blew out a hard breath of frustration and raked

a hand over his short hair. "Damn it, Maggie, don't do this."

"Do what?" She feigned ignorance.

He turned feral eyes on her, and Maggie could see he was only just holding his temper in check. "Don't shut me out and try to pretend this was just about sex. I know what you're doing."

Maggie blanched, but he had to be bluffing. He couldn't know her reasons for wanting to put some distance between them. Even now, with frustration radiating from every pore, he was so gorgeous and so supremely male that Maggie had to curl her fingers into her palms to keep from touching him.

"I'm not—" she began, but he cut her off with one warning look.

"We'll play it your way," he said, his voice low. "No strings, no commitments. I'll give you as much or as little as you want, okay?" He spread his arms wide, and Maggie swallowed hard at the sight he made. "I'm right here, and I'm not going anywhere. When you need me—day or night—I'll be waiting."

His words conjured up decadent images, and it was all Maggie could do not to plaster herself against all that heated muscle and beg him to take her back to bed. Suddenly, the thought of returning to the main house and her childhood bedroom, with only her old toys and stuffed animals to keep her company, seemed depressing.

As if sensing her wavering decision, Jack leaned forward. "C'mon, Mags. I'll light a fire in the fireplace. Have a glass of wine with me, and let's see where the night takes us."

Maggie knew very well where the night would take them if she decided to stay, but after a moment, she nodded. "Okay, I'll stay for a little bit," she finally said, eyeing him. "But only if you put some clothes on."

"Deal."

Jack made no effort to hide his grin, and Maggie felt an answering smile curve her lips at his obvious pleasure. She couldn't remember the last time a guy had been so anxious for her company, and she acknowledged that she liked the way it made her feel. She liked the way Jack made her feel, and that was what really scared her. The rational part of her brain told her to hightail it back to the main house and not let him pull her into his world. After all, she knew from experience that there was no place in that world for her.

8

JACK LISTENED AS Maggie slipped out of his bed at dawn the next morning, taking care not to disturb him. Knowing she wanted to leave without having to talk to him, he'd pretended to be asleep, but every cell in his body had been on high alert. He'd heard the soft rustle of her dress as she'd pulled it on, heard her barely muffled curse as she struggled with the zipper, and had been all too aware that she'd stood at the side of the bed and watched him for several long minutes, before she'd crept out of the cottage on bare feet.

Only when he heard the outer door close did he open his eyes and scrub his hands over his face. Glancing at the bedside clock, he saw it was barely 4:30 a.m. He'd spent most of the night awake, too aware of the woman beside him to sleep. He'd persuaded her to stay, and they'd watched a movie and had shared a bottle of wine, before she'd begun to sag with fatigue, leaning against his shoulder on the deep sofa. She'd protested when he'd carried her into his room and removed her dress, but as soon as she'd slid beneath the sheets, she'd fallen into a deep sleep. And as much as he'd wanted to wake her, he'd behaved like a gentleman. All night he'd listened to her soft breathing, felt her body heat seep into him and inhaled her delicate scent. It had taken all his restraint not to press himself against her, and wake her up with his mouth on her body.

Just the memory of what they'd shared last night gave him a boner, and with a groan he sat up and swung his legs out of bed. He had almost seven hours before he needed to be at the air base, but there was no way he'd get any sleep between now and then. The only thing that was going to make the morning easier was a long, cold shower.

He didn't know what Maggie's specific issues were, but he suspected that they went beyond her father, and guessed she'd been hurt pretty badly. He didn't know how to convince her that she was safe with him, except to let her call all the shots. He'd only known her for a couple of days, but everything about her appealed to him, and he'd never had the kind of sex that he'd had with Maggie Copeland.

Explosive.

He shouldn't be so surprised, but at thirty-three years old, he thought he was past the age where he could get a hard-on simply by looking at a woman. He suspected that he'd only touched the surface of Maggie's capacity for passion. He'd slept with his share of women, but he couldn't recall the last time he'd felt this need to get beneath a woman's skin and discover what made her tick. He wanted to know all Maggie's secrets, all her fantasies, all her dreams. But for now, at least, he'd give her the space she needed. He wouldn't pursue her, but he would let her come to him when she was ready. He just hoped he wouldn't have to wait too long.

MAGGIE HAD SPENT the morning on the mainland, in Bellingham, running errands and purchasing the supplies she'd need to get the darkroom operational again. She'd waited until noon to head back to Rocks Village, in order to avoid seeing Jack. She'd woken around dawn, completely disoriented, until she realized she was in Jack's bed. She'd had to disentangle herself from his heavy limbs, and he'd shifted restlessly as she'd climbed off the bed, but he hadn't woken.

After she'd dressed, Maggie had taken a selfish moment to just watch him. He'd lain naked and tangled in the bed linens, one arm bent over his head and his other resting on his stomach. The sheets had slipped to just below his navel, giving her a tantalizing glimpse of his happy trail, but hiding his credentials from view. Not that she needed to see him to recall exactly what he had hidden beneath the sheets.

She'd left in a hurry after that disturbing thought, in case her willpower deserted her. Now she turned her car down the private drive that led to the main house and saw Jack's Land Rover was gone. Telling herself that she didn't feel disappointed, Maggie gathered her bags and went into the house. But as she unpacked her purchases, her gaze continually drifted out the window and to the small cottage.

She couldn't stop thinking about the previous night and how he'd made love to her. He'd been so passionate, and yet tender, too. Even now, his touch seemed imprinted on her skin, and she only had to close her eyes to see his expression as he'd reached his release. She'd never encountered anyone quite like him before, and she'd be lying if she said she didn't want a repeat performance. He'd said he would give her whatever she wanted, whatever she needed, but Maggie was rapidly reaching the conclusion that what she wanted was the one thing he couldn't give her.

Gathering up her supplies, she made her way to the darkroom. What had once been a pantry off the kitchen had been transformed into a fully operational darkroom, complete with enlarger, safe light and a long table for her trays of chemicals. With digital photography becoming the norm, darkrooms were decreasing in popularity, but Maggie preferred to develop her own photos, especially when she was working with black-and-white film.

Now she opened the door and snapped on the light. The small room was amazingly clean, and Maggie knew her mother had kept it in good condition in the hopes that she would come home and want to stay. Despite the fact the room hadn't been used in years, the familiar scent of processing chemicals still lingered in the air, making Maggie feel nostalgic.

Setting her bags down on the nearest table, she walked the length of the room, taking in the equipment and supplies that she had left there ten years earlier. On an overhead shelf sat several cameras, two that her mother had given her, and one that she had purchased with her hard-earned babysitting money at the age of fifteen. By the time she was eighteen, she'd been able to afford something a little better. But she had left these cameras behind when she'd moved to Chicago. Seeing them now brought back memories of how she used to bike around the island, looking for the perfect photo op.

She paused in front of a set of drawers used to store her finished photos. Had her mother cleaned those out, as well, or were her youthful photos still there? Opening the first drawer, she pulled out a dozen packets of small note cards, carefully packaged in cellophane and sealed with a colorful sticker that read The Wonders of Whidbey by Maggie Copeland. Each packet contained eight different cards, each of which bore a different photo taken on Whidbey Island. They included a stunning sunset over Puget Sound, the Deception Pass bridge shrouded in mist and a group of harbor seals sunning themselves on a beach. She smiled in reminiscence, recalling her enthusiasm. Flipping through the photos, she had to admit they weren't half-bad.

Closing the drawer, she opened the next one and withdrew a sheaf of old photos. Her heart clenched as she saw the first picture, of Phillip Woodman. He was sitting on a large driftwood log, staring moodily out over the ocean, as if he had the weight of the world on his shoulders. In the next photo, he was laughing into the camera, having been cajoled out of his gloomy mood by Maggie. She remembered the day as if it was only yesterday.

Looking at the photo, Maggie didn't feel the heart-wrenching pain that she normally felt whenever she thought of Phillip. Her heart still ached, but it was more like a bruise that only hurt when poked. She wondered what Phillip was doing now, all these years later. Did he ever think of her? Did he—and his wife—still live on Whidbey Island? She'd never asked, and in the ten years since she'd left, nobody had ever volunteered the information.

With a sigh, she was about to replace the photos when one particular image caught her attention. Pulling the photo out of the stack, she tipped it toward the light, peering closely at it. She'd taken the picture when she'd been about fifteen years old. She and Eric had ridden their bikes to Cornet Bay, a tiny fishing village on the northern end of the island, bordered on either side by Deception State Park. She remembered how they had bought fried fish sandwiches at the local diner, and had walked out to the end of one of the piers. From there, one could see the majestic span of the Deception Pass bridge and watch the boats navigate the channel beneath.

Maggie had been dangling her feet in the water and fiddling with her camera when a charter boat had returned from a day at sea. Behind the boat, the sky had been orange, and a young man had stood on the bow as they steered toward the docks, ready to jump down and secure the lines. As the boat had neared the docks, he'd nodded toward Maggie. On impulse, she had snapped several pictures.

Now she stared at the photo, unwilling to believe the young man could be Jack Callahan. Swiftly, she turned to the tall supply cabinet and opened it, rummaging through the items until she found what she was looking for—a magnifying glass. Holding the photo beneath the light, she studied the picture again through the lens.

The quality wasn't great and the photo was the tiniest bit out of focus, but Maggie just about stopped breathing as she scrutinized the young man. He wore a pair of jeans and a blue sweatshirt, and he was younger and leaner than the Jack Callahan she knew, but there was no mistaking those broad shoulders or that careless grin. There was no doubt in Maggie's mind that she was looking at an image of Jack Callahan from thirteen years earlier. She didn't know his exact age, but guessed he would have been around nineteen or twenty at the time.

The realization that their paths had once crossed astounded her. Not only had their paths crossed, but she had also actually taken his picture! If she believed in destiny—which, thank goodness she didn't—she'd probably be a little freaked out right now. She recalled again the night they'd met, and her own vague sense of familiarity. Had she subconsciously recognized him from all those years ago?

The boat itself was big, almost fifty feet in length, and she could just make out the image of an older man in the pilot house. There were a dozen people standing on the open deck behind the cabin, mostly families with young kids.

Jack had said that he'd spent time on Whidbey Island as a kid, but she'd just assumed he'd come out here on vacation when he was really young, like twelve. She'd never have guessed that he worked on a charter boat, as the picture implied. Despite having grown up on the island, Maggie had only ever been out on a charter boat once, at the invitation of a friend, to see the killer whales. She'd been about sixteen, and it had been one of the most thrilling days of her life, watching them breach and frolic in the frigid waters.

"I'll be damned," she muttered, and slid the photo into the back pocket of her jeans.

For the next several hours, she occupied herself with setting up the darkroom and developing the film she had taken from that first night at Deception Pass. Her photos of the orca had come out surprisingly good, and Maggie had a deep sense of satisfaction as she clipped the wet photos to a drying wire and examined the results. The work was enjoyable and engrossing, but Maggie was aware that Jack Callahan was always at the back of her thoughts, waiting.

Just like he'd said he would be.

By the time she finally left the darkroom, the sun was sinking behind the trees, and long shadows were creeping over the property. It was just past six o'clock, and although Maggie told herself she wasn't checking up on him, she couldn't prevent herself from looking toward the cottage. The Land Rover was conspicuously absent, and Maggie tried to tell herself she didn't care. After all, it wasn't as if she was planning to knock on his door.

It was several hours later as Maggie stood at the kitchen counter, making herself a sandwich, when the sound of a car engine alerted her. Peering through the window, she watched as Jack's Land Rover drove slowly down the driveway and past the house. She could just make out his silhouette behind the wheel, before he pulled the vehicle to a stop near the cottage.

Unable to prevent herself, Maggie moved to the back door to watch him. It was several minutes before he finally got out of the Land Rover. He wore a pair of workout pants and a T-shirt, and he had a gym bag slung over one shoulder. He carried a paper grocery sack in his arm. She could make out a long loaf of crusty bread poking out of the top of the bag, and he carried a six-pack of beer in his free hand. He crossed the distance to the cottage, balancing the bag on one hip as he unlocked the door, but he never once glanced toward the main house. Even after he vanished inside, Maggie continued to watch until a light came on in the living area.

She couldn't help wondering what Jack had planned for dinner. A nice steak, probably. The cottage came equipped with a gas grill on the deck, and she could just imagine him kicking back with a cold beer as he fired up the barbecue. With a sigh, she turned back to the counter and eyed her tuna sandwich with distaste. Why hadn't she thought to do any food shopping while she'd been running errands? She'd just about gone through the few groceries that Eric and Danielle had left in the house.

Taking her plate, she moved into the living room where she wouldn't be tempted to spy on Jack. She told herself that what he did had nothing to do with her, and she certainly hadn't sunk so low that she'd invite herself over just because she was hungry—no matter how appetizing he might be. But when the tantalizing aroma of grilled steak wafted in through her open windows, she almost groaned aloud with defeat.

Pulling the photo from her back pocket, she studied it once more. "Well," she mused aloud, "at least it's an original excuse to go see him."

Gathering her courage, she followed the path to the cottage, hearing the soft strains of jazz music coming from inside. Wiping her hands nervously on the seat of her jeans, she raised her hand to knock and then hesitated. Was she being too forward? Had he meant what he said when he'd told her to come by anytime, day or night? Would he think she was completely pathetic because she couldn't stay away for even a day?

Before she could change her mind, the door opened, and Jack stood there, beer in hand. His eyes widened slightly in surprise before he smiled. The grin was so genuine that Maggie felt a wave of relief wash over her.

"I'm sorry," she blurted. "I hope you don't mind my coming over unannounced."

"Why would I mind?" he asked, and opened the door wider. "Come on in. I'm grilling up a couple of steaks, so you're just in time."

Maggie stepped inside, her embarrassment over barging in subsiding beneath his obvious pleasure. "Thanks, but you don't need to feed me. I don't want to be a nuisance."

He closed the door behind her, and gave her a tolerant look. "I *want* you to have dinner with me, Maggie.

In fact, I deliberately put on an extra steak on the off chance that you might stop by."

"Oh." She had no response to that, but couldn't deny the warm rush of satisfaction she felt at his words. "Well, thank you, but there's actually a reason for my visit."

"Okay, great," he said. "I can't wait to hear it, but in the meantime, let me get you something to drink. Wine, right?"

Maggie nodded. "Yes."

"Wait here," he commanded, and ducked into the kitchen. He returned to the living room scant moments later with a glass of wine. She indicated a collection of framed photos he'd arranged on the mantel. Most of them appeared to be of his family, but there were a couple that showed him standing next to his aircraft, in his flight suit.

"Is this your father?" Maggie asked, studying a photo of an older man.

"Yep. That's my old man, a career air-force pilot." He handed Maggie the glass of wine and she absently took a sip.

"And is this you as a little boy?" Maggie lifted down a photo to look at it more closely, and she couldn't keep the astonishment out of her voice. "You were so blond!"

Jack stood behind Maggie and looked at the photo. She was acutely aware of him, could feel his breath warming her neck and smell the unique scent that she'd come to associate with him. She was tempted to lean back against his solid frame, but held herself stiffly away, instead. All the while, her imagination surged with images of the previous night.

"Yeah," he said. "That's me when I was about twelve, and those are my grandparents. In fact, this picture was

taken not far from here. My grandfather owned a charter boat business and took people out on fishing trips,
or to see the orcas when they were migrating."

"Did you come out every summer?"

"You bet. My parents had just gotten divorced, and
my mom worked full-time. I think she worried that
I'd get into trouble without adult supervision, but she
couldn't afford to send me to summer camp. So my
grandparents paid for my airfare, and I spent the summer with them."

Maggie knew this was the perfect opening she'd been
waiting for to show him the photo she'd taken more
than ten years ago. But before she could say anything,
he caught her hand and pulled her toward the kitchen.

"Come sit out on the deck with me. I need to check
on the steaks."

Maggie followed him out to the deck, where two Adirondack chairs faced the water. He indicated Maggie
should sit down, and she watched as he lifted the grill
cover and turned the steaks. The aroma made her mouth
water, and she realized just how hungry she really was.

"You really did put on two steaks," she said with a
self-conscious laugh. "I hope I'm not that predictable."

"Well, I wasn't sure you'd come by, but a guy can
hope, right?" He gave her a smile that warmed her all
the way to her toes, and she took a hasty gulp of wine
to hide her reaction.

"So," she said, setting the glass down on the arm of
the chair. "Your grandfather had a charter business. Did
you go out on the boat with him?"

"Yep. I spent most of my teenage years on the water."

"And did you continue to come out here as you got
older? After you were in college, I mean?"

Closing the grill cover, Jack sat in the empty chair,

his legs sprawled so that his leg was nearly touching hers. "I did. My grandmother passed away while I was at the naval academy, and I lost my grandfather about six years ago." He gave her a rueful smile. "But at least he got to see me graduate, and he saw me fly."

"I'm sorry for your loss," Maggie said, knowing it was inadequate. "It sounds like you were very close to them."

"Yeah, there are days when I really miss them."

They were silent for several minutes. "So how did you end up flying jets? I would think you would have wanted to do something that kept you a little closer to the water, like the Coast Guard."

Jack laughed softly. "I thought of joining the Coast Guard, but my grandfather brought me to an air show when I was about thirteen years old, and as soon as I saw the jets, I knew that's what I wanted to do. Besides, there's nothing quite like landing a jet on an aircraft carrier in the middle of a pitching sea."

"Do you deploy often?" Maggie wanted to bite the words back as soon as she said them, but it was too late. She only hoped that her tone had been one of casual interest. She told herself it didn't matter if he deployed twelve months out of the year—she was leaving Whidbey Island in less than three weeks, and Jack Callahan would be nothing more than a pleasant memory.

But when she glanced at him, she saw his attention had sharpened on her, as if he suspected her question was more than just neighborly interest.

"I've done four sea deployments," he said carefully, "and I'll probably do at least one more while I'm stationed at Whidbey. Why?"

She shrugged. "No reason. I just wondered. How long are you usually gone?"

"It depends on the mission. A typical deployment lasts anywhere between three and six months. But my squadron isn't coming up for a sea deployment for at least another few months, and you've already said you're returning to Chicago in a few weeks, so a deployment would have no impact on us." He leaned forward in his chair to look directly into her eyes. "What's going on, Maggie?"

Maggie felt herself flush. "Nothing. I was just making conversation. Shouldn't you check on the steaks?"

Setting his beer down, Jack rose to his feet in one fluid movement and opened the grill. "Good call," he said. "We're ready to eat." He gave her a look that clearly said he wasn't finished with their conversation, before transferring the steaks to a plate and carrying them into the kitchen.

Maggie followed him inside and watched as he quickly set the table. "What can I do?"

Jack indicated the loaf of bread that she had seen him carrying earlier. "You can slice the bread, and I made a salad. It's in the fridge if you want to grab it."

Maggie did as he asked, struck by the cozy intimacy of the scene. As she placed the salad on the table, Jack snagged a cherry tomato from the bowl and popped it into his mouth, smiling at her from around it. She felt herself smiling back, even as self-doubt began to creep in. He hadn't once referred to the previous night, or given her any indication that he expected—or even wanted—a repeat performance.

They sat down, and Jack raised his glass to hers. She liked the deep indents that appeared in his cheeks when he smiled. Hell, she liked the way his eyes crinkled, and the way they seemed to dance with inner amusement. He'd lit a fat candle in the center of the table, and she realized his eyes were hazel, more gold than brown right now, with a dark ring around the iris. Why hadn't she noticed that before?

"To many more evenings just like this," he said, touching the rim of his beer glass against her wine goblet.

Maggie smiled uncertainly back at him. "Well, at least while I'm here."

"You bet," he responded, and grinned at her before taking a hefty swallow of his beer. He seemed unconcerned by her words and the implication that she would eventually leave Whidbey Island. Maybe he was relieved that their relationship wouldn't extend beyond three weeks. Maybe he was one of those guys who had a woman in every port, and he didn't want a long-term commitment.

She watched as he ate, enthusiasm evident in the way he savored every bite. "Is it good?"

"You tell me." He looked meaningfully at her untouched plate.

Maggie sliced off a tender bit of steak and put it in her mouth, and her eyes closed in pleasure. "Oh, my God," she said, chewing, "this is absolutely fabulous."

Jack grinned, pleased. "I may not be a culinary whiz, but I do know how to grill. You said earlier that there was a reason for your visit. Please say you didn't stop by just to tell me you've arranged for a plumber, or some such nonsense. I told you that I can take care of that, Mags."

Maggie liked the way he shortened her name, suggesting a familiarity that she wasn't completely comfortable with, but enjoyed all the same.

"No," she said, putting down her utensils. "It's noth-

ing like that. It's actually a pretty unbelievable story—
a coincidence, if you will."

"Oh, yeah? I don't much believe in coincidences,
but let's hear it."

Reaching into her back pocket, Maggie pulled out
the photo, holding it so that he couldn't immediately
see the image.

"I was in my darkroom today, developing the pictures of the orca whale that we saw that first night at
Deception Pass." He nodded and continued to watch
her expectantly. "So, I haven't used the darkroom in
over ten years, and I was going through some of the
drawers where I store old photos. I came across this
one photo that I took as a teenager. I think I was about
fifteen years old."

Drawing a deep breath, Maggie handed him the picture, aware that her hand trembled. He watched her intently for a long moment, before dropping his attention
to the photo. Maggie watched as he studied the image,
his brows drawing together, before his eyes widened in
surprised recognition. He snapped his gaze back to hers.

"Is this what I think it is? Jesus, where did you say
you got this?"

"I took it a long time ago, at Cornet Bay. Eric and I
had ridden our bikes out there and were just hanging
out on the pier. I watched this boat come into the harbor, and there was this guy standing on the bow. He
nodded to me, so I snapped a couple of pictures." She
bit her lip. "Do you remember that day?"

Jack looked at the photo again and nodded. "I do,
actually. That was the last time I went out on that boat.
I left two days later to go back to school and didn't return to Whidbey Island for a couple of years. In the

meantime, my grandfather sold the charter business and retired. So yeah, I remember that day really well."

Do you remember me?

For one horrified second, Maggie feared she'd uttered the words aloud. She had to bite her lip to keep from asking him, telling herself that, of course, he wouldn't remember some kid sitting on a dock, nearly thirteen years earlier. Why would he? She hadn't even remembered him until she'd found the photo.

"How old were you?" she asked, instead.

"I'd just turned twenty. I was entering my third year at the academy, and I remember how hard it was leaving the island that summer. It was almost like I knew that would be the last time Gramps and I went out together. I was right." He smoothed a finger over the picture. "Do you mind if I keep this? It would mean a lot to me."

"No, of course I don't mind. I wasn't even sure it was you," she fibbed. "I mean, the photo isn't the greatest quality."

"Oh, that's me all right. And I can just see my grandfather inside the cabin. The boat was called the *Prince of Whales,* and Gramps had an almost perfect record of sighting an orca every time he went out. And if he didn't see an orca, he either gave folks their money back or offered to go out again another day at no additional charge."

"Ah, so that's how you know so much about orcas," Maggie said. "I wondered. Some coincidence, don't you think?"

"I already told you, Mags. I don't believe in coincidences."

9

JACK TOOK ANOTHER bite of his steak as he watched Maggie squirm. He still couldn't believe she'd taken a photo of him all those years ago, or that she'd kept it. He'd told her the truth when he'd said he didn't believe in coincidences. Call him crazy, but he'd say it was destiny.

While he remembered the day that photo had been taken, he had no memory of Maggie. She'd said she'd been on the pier, but he couldn't recall seeing a teenaged girl on the docks that day. She'd said she was only fifteen at the time, so it was no wonder he hadn't noticed her. At twenty, he'd considered himself a man. He wouldn't have had any interest in a high school girl, although he wished he could remember seeing her. He would have liked to know what she looked like as a long-limbed, gawky kid with wide eyes and all that wild hair.

Now she played with her salad, stirring her fork through the greens. "So what are you saying?" she finally asked. "That because our paths crossed once, that we're destined for each other?"

"They crossed three times, Maggie. Once when you

took that photo, once when we met on the beach and again when I rented this cottage. That's more than just coincidence."

Maggie stared at him dubiously. "It's an island, Jack. I've probably crossed paths several times with a dozen different people, but that doesn't make any of them my soul mate. I think it's cool that I took that photo of you, but it doesn't mean anything."

"Maybe," he said smoothly. "But I'm pretty sure you didn't have an immediate attraction to any of those other people, or have incredibly hot sex with them, either. I'm just guessing." Smiling at her shocked expression, he took another bite of steak.

At least she didn't claim that the sex hadn't meant anything, as he'd half expected her to. He wouldn't have believed her, since he was absolutely certain she was incapable of having meaningless sex, even if she tried to convince herself otherwise. He watched in satisfaction as color seeped into her neck and slowly traveled to her face. After a moment, she dropped her gaze and concentrated on her food. Jack didn't feel any remorse for having embarrassed her. Hell, he wanted her thinking about incredibly hot sex, with him. Only with him. Even now, he wanted her.

She'd worn her hair loose over her shoulders, and he couldn't help but wonder if it was because he'd said he preferred it that way. It fell in long, loopy ringlets around her face, and for once she didn't try to push it back behind her ears. She wore a pair of jeans and a sleeveless, button-down blouse that showed off her toned arms. She looked good enough to eat, and Jack had to force himself to concentrate on his meal, and not let her see how much her presence affected him.

He still couldn't believe she'd shown up at his door

tonight. He'd figured she'd stay away from him for at least two or three days while she mentally beat herself up over having slept with him. He hid his smile behind his beer glass. Now that she was here, there was no way he was letting her leave, at least not before he'd had a chance to make love to her again.

"So, um, what do you do when you're not actually flying jets?" she asked.

The obvious answer was that he had sex with her, and he had to bite the words back. But his response must have been evident in his expression, because her eyes widened and she took a hasty swallow of her wine. "I mean, of course, when you're on duty," she added.

"Well, I have collateral duties as an operations officer," he said, "which keeps me pretty busy when I'm not actually flying."

"So how many hours do you actually spend flying?"

Jack shrugged. "I'm trained to fly from an aircraft carrier, but we obviously can't be out at sea one hundred percent of the time. So while I'm here, I perform one or two flights per day. Each flight will last about two hours, but there's a lot of prep work involved. The debrief only takes about thirty minutes, and then I have four or five hours to perform my collateral duties, take a break, go chow down, or whatever. If I'm scheduled for a second flight, then the whole routine starts all over again. The battle rhythm is a little different when we're actually on a carrier, but that's essentially it in a nutshell."

"Are you glad you became a pilot? Do you ever feel as if you've sacrificed something for your dream? I mean, you've obviously made a choice to put your career over a family, right?"

Ah. Now they were getting somewhere. Is that what

she really believed? That military guys didn't make good husbands or fathers? It made sense, given her own history, and how her father had behaved. Hell, even his own dad had spent more time with the air force than he had with his family. The result was that his mother had had an affair, and his parents had eventually divorced. At twelve years old, his entire life had been turned upside down. Following the divorce, he'd been shipped off to Whidbey Island every summer. He'd loved those months he spent with his grandparents, but he'd been determined not to follow his father's example. He fully intended to be a good husband. He'd made a promise to himself that if he ever married, he'd never be unfaithful, and he'd never give his wife a reason to turn to another man. He just hadn't met a woman he'd wanted to commit a lifetime to.

Until now.

He couldn't explain what it was about Maggie Copeland that called to him, but she appealed to him on a level that went deeper than mere sexual attraction. She appealed to him on a gut level. As soon as he'd seen her on the beach, something in him had recognized her, and responded. Maybe, subconsciously, he did remember her from that day on the dock. All he knew was that he couldn't stop thinking about her.

Physically, they were as perfect together as two people could be. Now he just had to convince her not to return to Chicago, or at least stay on Whidbey Island long enough to see that they could have a good thing together. Did he want to marry her? He wasn't nearly ready to make that call, but he did know that he wanted to settle on Whidbey Island permanently. As much as he'd enjoyed growing up in Boulder, Colorado, he needed to be near the ocean, and coming back to Whidbey Island had felt like coming home.

"I wouldn't say I've chosen my career over a family," he finally responded. "I'm only thirty-three, Maggie, so I still have time to meet someone and settle down. And as far as having sacrificed something? Absolutely not. I consider it an honor to fly for the navy. I've been doing it for twelve years, and I love it, but I've actually started to think about what I'd like to do beyond flying jets."

"And what have you thought about?"

"That I'd like to start a charter business here on Whidbey Island, but instead of boats, I'd have a couple of small planes. I'd take folks back and forth to the other islands, or even to British Columbia."

Maggie considered him for a moment. "You really want to settle here permanently?"

"Oh, yeah. I've known for years that this is where I want to raise a family. My grandparents left me some land just north of Oak Harbor, and I've already hired an architect to design a house for me."

Maggie looked at him in surprise. "Wow. That's great," she finally said, but her words lacked the ring of sincerity. "Where exactly is the property located?"

"The lot overlooks Cornet Bay, not far from where this photo was taken. I decided to do a traditional post-and-beam-style house. Sort of seems appropriate, given the location."

"I agree. That whole part of the island is lovely."

"It sure is. I'll take you out to the site one afternoon so you can see it for yourself. With your artistic eye, maybe you can give me some pointers on how to situate the house on the property in order to take advantage of the views." He grinned. "I may also get a small place in California, say near La Jolla Beach, since I do love to ride a board, but that would be strictly for vacations."

Maggie's voice sounded a little weak. "It sounds like you've given this a lot of thought."

"Oh, I have." Jack paused. "What about you? Is Chicago where you want to be permanently?"

He watched in fascination as a series of emotions flitted across her face. Uncertainty, distress, determination.

"I'm not sure," she finally said, raising her chin a little. "I've been out there for almost ten years, and I'm finally getting my own photography business up and running. I have a cute little place in Lincoln Park, but there are definitely times when I feel like a fish out of water."

"And your clientele includes new brides who likely won't make it to their tenth wedding anniversary, isn't that what you told me?"

Maggie flashed him a resentful look. "Do you remember everything I told you?"

He grinned, unabashed. "You bet. What I don't get, though, is that you seemed so genuinely happy taking photographs of that orca whale, and I'll bet good money that the pictures came out fantastic."

Maggie shrugged, but Jack could see his words pleased her. "They did come out well, actually. I developed them earlier today, and I got one photo of the whale coming almost completely out of the water. The detail is pretty incredible. So yes, I did enjoy taking those photos, but what does that have to do with anything?"

"Well, I'd think you could make a killing selling your wildlife photos. Whidbey Island is where you grew up, where your roots are. Your brother is here, and it sounds like your mother still comes back here. I guess I'm just surprised that you don't want to settle down here."

Maggie gave him a baleful look. "Not all my memories of Whidbey Island are as idyllic as yours, Jack."

"Maybe you just need to create some new memories." He waggled his eyebrows meaningfully, but Maggie didn't smile.

"I couldn't wait to get off this island."

Jack leaned forward. "But now that you're back, you can't tell me that you're not the tiniest bit happy?"

Maggie looked at him, and then away. "Of course I am," she acknowledged reluctantly. "A lot has changed in ten years. I love being back in the shop, working with Carly, and it feels good to be home."

Jack was careful not to let her see the satisfaction he felt at her words. Just the fact that she used the word *home* gave him hope that perhaps she didn't dislike Whidbey Island as much as she professed.

"But you can't see yourself living here on a permanent basis?" he persisted.

"I don't know, Jack." She sounded resigned. "I've only been back for a couple of days. Yes, it feels good to be home, but that doesn't mean I want to stay. I know there are all kinds of reasons to do so, not the least being that my new nieces or nephews will be living here. But could I really making a living out of shooting wildlife? And do I even want to? I just don't know."

"People get married on Whidbey Island, too," Jack said gently. "You could probably establish a clientele for your wedding photography here, the same as you did in Chicago. Who knows…the brides out here might be a little more grounded than your Chicago socialites."

To his surprise, Maggie pushed away from the table and surged to her feet. "Okay, you're beginning to freak me out a little. You sound like everyone else who wants me to come back to Whidbey Island. I know that on the surface there seem to be a million reasons why I would want to leave Chicago and settle here, but it's not that easy, okay? I wish I could explain it to you, but I can't, and I hope you won't ask." Looking around a little frantically, she pushed her hair back from her face, and Jack saw with a sense of shock that she was close to tears.

"Maggie—"

"Don't." She raised a hand to forestall whatever he might have said next. "Thank you for dinner. I'm sorry to be rude, but I have to go."

Jack had risen to his feet as soon as she'd stood up, and now he rounded the table to grasp her by the shoulders. "Maggie, don't go. Look, I'm sorry. I didn't mean to upset you, believe me. Please don't go, not like this."

She brushed a hand over her eyes and gave him a tremulous smile. "It's not you, it's me. That's the standard response, right? Look, I appreciate what you're trying to do, but I really do need to leave."

She broke free from his grasp and fled the house, leaving Jack to stare after her in bemusement. He heard the front door slam, and he could picture her running back up the path to the main house.

He felt like a complete dick. He'd only wanted her to acknowledge that there were positive aspects to life on Whidbey Island, not cause her to have an emotional meltdown. He dragged in a deep breath and scrubbed his hands over his face, trying to decide what to do next. She might not welcome his intrusion, but he wouldn't be able to relax until he checked on her. As much as he wanted to go after her immediately, he knew she'd need some time to compose herself.

Hating himself for having caused her distress, he finally left the cottage and sprinted along the walk and knocked lightly on the back door. The kitchen was completely dark, and there was no answer. Stepping off the porch, Jack checked that Maggie's car was still in the driveway, and then glanced at the second floor of the house. All the windows were dark, with no sign that anyone was home. He couldn't believe she would have gone anywhere on foot, not at this hour, when the sun had already set. He suspected she was in her bedroom and was deliberately not answering his knock.

Returning to the back door, he let himself into the kitchen and was just making his way toward the front staircase, when a flickering light at the back of the kitchen drew his attention. A red lightbulb was fixed over a closed door, and Jack realized this was the darkroom she had spoken of earlier. Instinctively, he knew she would be inside, and knocked softly on the panels.

"Maggie? It's Jack. Can I come in?"

"Is the light on in the kitchen?" Her voice was muffled.

"No," he answered. "It's completely dark out here."

He heard her moving around on the other side of the door, and then it opened just enough for her to reach out and yank him into the room, before she closed the door behind them.

"I'm developing some prints and the tiniest amount of light could ruin the process," she explained.

It took a moment for Jack's eyes to adjust to the muted red lighting inside the room. At the far end of the room, there was a long table, and he could see a deep sink, and several large trays of liquid that had a distinctly chemical odor. Floor-to-ceiling shelves stood to his left, bearing all kinds of supplies and equipment. Another table took up part of the wall to his right, where a large piece of equipment stood next to a tall cabinet of slender drawers. Several lengths of wire had been strung across the room, and photos hung from them like wet laundry on a clothesline.

"Wow," he said, impressed in spite of himself. "I've never been inside a darkroom before. You actually know how to use all this stuff?"

"Well, it's not like operating a fighter jet," she said, and sounded amused.

Jack finally looked at her, relieved to see that his fears hadn't been realized. She wasn't crying, and she didn't look angry with him. If anything, she looked as if she'd been expecting him. And she'd worried that she was the predictable one. He gave a snort of laughter.

"What's so funny?" she asked.

"You." Without giving her a chance to protest, he took her by the arms and pulled her close to him, studying her face in the eerie light of the red lightbulb. She watched him warily, but made no move to pull away. "I want to apologize again for what happened at dinner. I behaved like an ass, and I'm sorry. I just—" He broke off, uncertain how to continue.

"You just—what?" she asked softly.

He blew out a hard breath. "I just like you so damned much, and I can't stand the thought of you leaving in less than three weeks. It was unfair of me to pressure you the way I did, and I'm sorry."

Maggie stroked a hand down his chest and ducked her head. "No, it was actually really sweet of you. I overreacted, and I'm sorry I ran out on you." Looking back up at him, she gave him a small smile. "I like you, too, and while Chicago might not be perfect for me, I'm not sure Whidbey Island is, either. But I'm not ready to make any decisions about my future. Not yet. I just need you to know that."

It wasn't what Jack wanted to hear, but he knew better than to argue with her right now. Instead, he slid his hands beneath her hair and smoothed his thumbs across her cheeks.

"I get it," he assured her. "I'll stop promoting the virtues of life on Whidbey Island. But I won't stop trying to convince you to stay."

"Oh, yeah?" Her gaze dropped to his mouth, and just like that the air between them changed. "What methods did you have in mind?"

"I thought I'd start with this," he murmured, and knew she could feel his heart thumping hard beneath her palm as he dipped his head and kissed her, a soft, sweet kiss that he hoped conveyed just how he felt about her.

To his delight, she returned the kiss with a fervent passion, as if she was afraid he might change his mind.

As if.

No freaking way was he about to do that. He deepened the kiss, sliding his hands around to her back and pulling her fully against his body. She tasted like sweet wine, and he wanted to devour her. She made a sound of approval in her throat and wound her arms around his neck, tunneling her fingers through his hair.

This is what he'd thought of all day; this woman in his arms, her mouth beneath his, her body responding to him because she couldn't help herself. She could fool herself into thinking she didn't want to return to her childhood home, but she couldn't fool herself about the connection they had.

She broke the kiss, pushing back enough to get her hands beneath his T-shirt and push it upward. Jack helped her by reaching behind his head to grasp a handful of fabric and drag the shirt off. Maggie's hands were everywhere, touching and exploring whatever part of him she could reach. Jack reciprocated by unfastening the buttons on her blouse until it fell open, revealing the white bra she wore underneath. It wasn't an erotic undergarment by any stretch of the imagination, but the sight of her smooth, pale flesh was a complete turn-on, and Jack thought he'd never seen a woman look as sexy in a simple bra as she did.

"Take this off," he said, his voice gruff.

Maggie complied, shrugging the shirt off until she stood in just her jeans and bra. Jack stroked the back of his knuckles along the side of her neck and over the fragile line of her collarbone, lingering on the small pulse that thrummed frantically at the base of her throat.

"Are you nervous?"

She shook her head. "No. Yes."

Jack laughed softly. "Come here."

"Wait. I want to see you." Her hands went to the snap on his jeans, unfastening it with fingers that trembled. She slid the zip down, and then pushed both his jeans and the boxers down over his hips, freeing his erection. With a soft "oh" of admiration, she curled her fingers around him, squeezing gently. Jack groaned and leaned back, gripping the edge of the table for support.

"Maggie…"

"Does that feel good?" She slid one hand over him, stroking his length. She smoothed her free hand over his abdomen and chest, even as she leaned forward and placed teasing kisses along his jaw and the seam of his lips. "Because it feels good to me."

"Oh, yeah," he breathed, watching her. "That feels incredible."

"Good. Because ever since last night, all I've been

able to think about is you…of being with you again."
She dragged her lips along the side of his throat, causing him to shudder lightly with sensation. "I know I shouldn't, because it's not fair to either of us, but I just can't help myself."

"What's not fair is that you're still dressed," he managed to say through gritted teeth. "I want to be inside you, Maggie."

"Do you have protection?" Her voice was breathy and high.

Jack cursed softly. He hadn't even thought about bringing a condom with him. He hadn't planned this; had only wanted to make sure she was okay. "I can run back to the cottage," he said, lightly running his hands over her cheeks and ears. "It'll only take a minute."

"I don't want to wait that long," she protested. "I want you now."

"You're killing me," Jack groaned. "We can't—"

"Shh," she said, and raised herself up to press a soft, moist kiss against his mouth. "Trust me."

Jack stared at her for a moment, and then sagged back against the table, surrendering himself to her. "I trust you," he replied.

Her smile was one of satisfaction and anticipation as she pressed a kiss against the center of his chest and slowly began working her way down his body, touching him lightly with her lips and tongue. When he realized her intent, lust ricocheted through him, causing him to swell even more beneath her fingers.

She was crouched in front of him now, holding him in her hand as she looked up at him. "Tell me what you like," she whispered. "I want to make this good for you."

"Sweetheart," he rasped, "this is already so good, I'm on the verge of losing it."

Maggie smiled up at him, and then turned her attention to his arousal. "I want to taste you." Dipping her head, she delicately ran her tongue over the blunt head of his penis, and he jerked against her palm. "Mmm. You taste good."

His breathing was coming faster as she took him in her mouth and swirled her tongue around him. The hot, slick sensation around his cock was so intense that Jack had to grit his teeth to maintain control. When she began to suck on him in concert with the stroking motion of her fist, Jack knew he wasn't going to last long.

"Easy, baby," he panted.

Maggie broke free long enough to give him a seductive look from beneath her lashes. "I want you to come."

At the raw sexuality in her eyes, pressure built in his balls and his dick swelled even more. He was such a goner, but he didn't want this to end so soon, not without giving her pleasure in return.

"Wait," he gasped, and thrusting his fingers into her hair, gently drew her away from him. "There's something I need to do first. Come up here."

She rose to her feet, running her tongue over her lips as if savoring the taste of him. Reaching behind her, Jack unfastened her bra and slowly drew it free of her arms to let it fall on the floor. Then he filled his hands with her breasts, lifting their weight in his palms and running his thumbs over her nipples. She was the perfect size, and her areolas were large and pink, the nipples drawing to tight points beneath his fingertips. Lifting one breast, he bent his head and flicked his tongue over the distended tip, drawing a gasp from Maggie. When he drew it into his mouth and sucked hard, she thrust her fingers into his hair and held his head there, her breath warm against his ear.

"Oh, that feels so good," she moaned. "Don't stop."

Jack didn't intend to. As he laved her breast, he used his free hand to work the button on her jeans, opening them enough to slide a hand into the back and cup her rear, kneading the pliant flesh.

"Take these off," he muttered, releasing her breast to help her push the denim down over her hips.

"My shoes," she said on a broken laugh, bending to unfasten the laces. "My pants are stuck."

"Here, let me help."

Before she could protest, he picked his shirt up off the floor and laid it on the table, and then turning Maggie, he lifted her onto the surface so that her legs, still trapped in her pants, dangled over the edge. His own jeans were still down around his knees, and he took a brief moment to kick off his shoes and step out of his pants and boxers.

"Now it's your turn," he said, infusing the words with wicked promise, as he pulled her shoes and socks from her feet and then dragged her jeans and panties down the length of her legs. Finally, she was completely naked. "Much better," he purred, his eyes devouring her.

In the eerie red light of the dark room, she looked like every fantasy he'd ever had. Her breasts rose and fell rapidly with her agitated breathing, and she watched him with an overtly sensual expression that caused his balls to tighten in anticipation.

"Here," he said, moving between her splayed legs, "slide to the edge of the table. I've got you. Comfortable?"

She was leaning back on her hands, and now she nodded, biting her lip. "Yes. What are you going to do?"

Jack smiled. "Anything I want." He started by smoothing his hands over her stomach and hips, and then back up to her breasts to toy briefly with her nipples. Then he crouched in front of her, and slowly drew her knees wide. "This is what I want," he said, aware that his voice was husky with desire.

In the dim light, she looked achingly feminine and mysterious, and Jack couldn't resist pressing a kiss, first to her knee, and then to the soft skin of her inner thigh.

"You're trembling," he observed. "Are you cold?"

"No. Just…completely turned on."

Jack understood, and it took all his restraint not to stand up and thrust himself into her body. Instead, he slid his fingers over her, gratified when she gave a soft, broken cry, and jerked convulsively. Even in the indistinct light, he could see she was swollen with arousal and glistening with moisture.

"You're so wet," he said on a note of wonder. Parting her lips, he swirled his finger over the small rise of her clitoris. She groaned and pushed her hips against his hand, seeking more of the intimate contact. "Do you like that?"

"Oh, God," she panted. "I like it too much."

Holding her open with his fingers, Jack leaned in and licked her, stroking his tongue over her opening, and teasing her clitoris as she made small mewling sounds and writhed beneath him. He used his tongue to thrust into her, while stroking her with his fingers, and he felt her muscles begin to draw in and tighten.

"That's it, baby," he breathed against her aroused flesh. "Come for me."

"Jack," she cried, and grasped his head with surprising strength. "Come inside me. Now, please!"

Jack looked up the length of her body to find her watching him with wild eyes. Her breathing was ragged and he could see she was on the very edge of control.

"Babe," he protested, "you know I want to, but—"

"I'm safe," she said, her voice almost frantic. "I'm on the Pill, and I'm completely safe. I just—I *need* you inside me."

Hearing the urgency in her voice, and seeing the evidence of her arousal, Jack was a complete goner. There was nothing he wanted more than to bury himself in her heat, but he tried one last time to reason with her.

"I'm safe, too, but, Maggie—"

"Please, Jack!"

With a groan of utter defeat, Jack surged to his feet and grasped his cock in his hand, fitting the wide head to her entrance. Maggie was on her elbows, her legs wrapped around his hips as she used her heels to urge him on. Gritting his teeth against the exquisite sensation, he eased himself into her, feeling her flesh grasp at him. She was tight and hot, and Jack knew the ride was going to be fast and hard. Sliding his hands beneath her buttocks, he lifted her for a better fit.

"Hold on," he said hoarsely, and began pumping into her, so deep that his balls ached with the need for release. Her body fisted around him, her hands gripping his wrists as she rose to meet each powerful thrust.

"Oh, yes, yes…" she cried, her body tightening around him. "Oh, Jack, I'm going to!"

Reaching between their bodies, Jack found her clitoris and stroked it hard, watching her face contort in pleasure as she curled forward, her fingers digging into his wrists as her body shuddered with the force of her orgasm. With the last vestiges of his control, he snatched himself free from her body and fisted his cock, stroking himself twice before he came in a blinding, white-hot rush of ecstasy, spilling himself onto her stomach and breasts in long, hot spurts.

For several long minutes, there was only the sound of their harsh breathing in the small room. Jack had never felt so completely drained. Maggie lay half sprawled beneath him, her breasts heaving as she sucked in lungfuls of air. Her glorious hair spilled around her on the table as she watched him through sated, slumberous eyes.

"Thank you," she said softly. "You have no idea how much I needed that."

Jack laughed softly; he couldn't help himself. She was thanking him for the most powerful release he'd ever experienced. Even their lovemaking of the previous night, while amazing, hadn't been like this. He watched as she raised one hand and languidly traced a finger through the pearly fluid on her stomach. Incredibly, the sight made Jack's dick twitch.

"Here, stay still while I find something to clean us up with," he advised, looking around the small room.

"There are some paper towels on the back wall," Maggie said, "and the sink has running water."

Several minutes later, when they were both clean and dry, Jack helped Maggie get dressed, before pulling on his own clothes. He turned her toward him and lifted her face with a finger under her chin.

"I'm sorry about that," he murmured. "That was ridiculously rushed, and not very romantic. I just didn't want to take a chance and come inside of you."

Maggie's eyes widened. "Are you kidding me? That was the most intense experience I've ever had, and that's saying something, because I thought last night was unbelievable." She smiled softly and wound her arms around his waist, stretching up to plant a moist kiss against his mouth. "Watching you come like that was the most incredibly sexy thing I've ever seen. I may never let you use a condom again."

Jack grinned and hauled her against his chest, kissing her hard. He definitely liked the sound of that.

_10_

WITH JUST THREE days until the arts-and-crafts festival, the town of Coupeville was already gearing up for the thousands of tourists who would flock to the area to enjoy the celebration.

Maggie had dragged their exhibit tent out of storage and checked to ensure it had no rips or other damage. The weather prediction was for clear, sunny skies, and Maggie was grateful they wouldn't have to contend with any rain or drizzle. Not only did that tend to drive away customers, but it was also no fun for the artisans who were trying to sell their products, either.

They had spent the past two days selecting the items that they would sell in the tent, versus the shop, including a variety of hand-blown glass decorations.

"I think we're ready," Maggie declared, looking over the items that they had set aside.

The festival would feature well over three hundred exhibitors, whose tents would extend along the entire length of the waterfront. In addition, there would be an antiques market, wine-tasting events, attractions for the children and evening concerts. The annual fair was the biggest event of the year, not just on Whidbey Island, but in the entire Pacific Northwest. Despite the fact she hadn't helped prepare for a festival in over ten years, Maggie found herself falling into the familiar routine as if it had only been yesterday.

"It seems so strange to be getting ready for the festival without Eric or my mom," Maggie mused.

Carly looked up from where she was redecorating the front window of the shop and gave her a wistful smile. "Every year for the past ten years, I've heard Eric and your mother say the same thing about you. It just never felt the same getting ready for the festival without you. You always looked forward to it so much, and you had more inventory to sell than most of the other exhibitors at the fair."

Maggie ducked her head. "Well, I promise you that's not the case this year."

Her photos of the orca whale had come out astonishingly well, but with just three days until the festival, Maggie couldn't decide how to present them. Did she want to sell them as postcards, or note cards, or as framed photos? She had little time to decide, and a lot of work to do if she wanted to produce enough copies to make selling them worthwhile. The festival tended to attract a wealthy clientele, and sales over the three-day event often outnumbered the sales they did for the entire year. Which was why Eric had begged Maggie to come back to help oversee the preparations, and ensure their success. This year, as in previous years, their tent would be situated near the shop, which would make it easy to invite interested patrons to browse their extended line of sea-glass jewelry.

"Well, I heard this morning that you can't find a vacant room anywhere on the island," Carly commented.

"That's good news, considering the economy. I'm thinking this might be one of the best festivals yet. I hope you're able to get some of your work on display, hon. Talent like yours should be shared."

Her words were almost identical to what Jack had said to her in the darkroom four days ago. After they'd engaged in the hottest sex she'd ever imagined, and had been preparing to leave the darkroom, Jack had spotted the photos she'd taken of the orca whale. There were several of the sunset beyond the headland, and even one of Jack, standing in silhouette against the brilliant sky, although she didn't recall seeing him there as she'd snapped the picture. She'd been completely focused on the wash of colors reflected in the water. When she'd developed the film and realized she'd taken yet another photo of him, she'd wondered if the universe was trying to send her a message. But what kind of message? To turn and run like hell in the other direction? Or to open her arms and welcome what she couldn't seem to avoid? Right now, she was equally torn between the two options.

"How's that pilot of yours doing?" Carly asked, as if she could read Maggie's thoughts.

"Jack? Oh, he's fine," she responded automatically.

"Yes, he is," Carly said in obvious satisfaction. "He is very fine, if you ask me. Is he coming to pick you up again this afternoon?"

"Er, no. I drove my car into town this morning. And he's not *my pilot*."

"That's too bad. He sure is a looker. And a gentleman, too." She gave Maggie a wink. "And talk about convenient. What I couldn't do with a yard ornament like that in my backyard!"

"Carly!" Maggie pretended to be shocked, but

couldn't prevent giggling at the other woman's outrageous remark.

"Seriously, though, it looked to me like you two had a connection. Was I wrong?"

Maggie felt herself going warm beneath Carly's knowing look. She shook her head. "No, you weren't wrong. There's definitely a…connection."

"So why do you look so depressed? If I had a guy like that looking at me the way he looks at you, I'd be turning cartwheels down Main Street."

Maggie sighed. "I know that's what I should be doing, but there's no future in it for us. He's stuck here for at least the next three years, and I live in Chicago. He's in the navy, which means long sea deployments and…all the rest of the baggage that goes with being in the military. I'm not sure I'm ready for that again. That last relationship broke me, Carly. Jack deserves better than me."

Carly put her hands on her hips and leveled a steady look at Maggie. "Is that really what you believe? That you're broken?" She gave a snort and gestured around the shop. "In case you haven't noticed, that's our specialty."

Maggie glanced at the display cases full of sea-glass jewelry and frowned. "What do you mean?"

Stepping forward, Carly took Maggie's hands in her own. "Don't you see? You're like this sea glass. You started out whole, and then you got broken. You traveled around, got tumbled against the rocks a bit and all those sharp edges got smoothed out. Now you're back on the same shore where you started, but you're different…you're more beautiful and special than you ever were before."

Maggie felt the prick of tears behind her eyelids, and

leaned down to give Carly a fierce hug. "Thank you. I never thought of it like that before."

"It's true," Carly said. She stepped away and gave Maggie a thoughtful look. "Have you ever considered coming back? I know you think you don't want to live here, but in the time you've been back, I've seen a huge change in you. You came here with the weight of the world on your shoulders, looking as if you hadn't seen the sun in ten years, and hadn't had a decent meal in all that time, either." She gestured expansively. "Now look at you, letting your hair down, a little color back in your cheeks and I've never seen anyone devour a pizza the way you did at lunch today."

Maggie flushed. Everything Carly said was true. Since she'd met Jack—since she'd started sleeping with Jack—she felt like a different woman.

Four days had passed since their interlude in the darkroom, and as if by unspoken agreement, Maggie found herself at Jack's door each evening after he returned home. Sometimes she would bring dinner with her, sometimes Jack would prepare a meal, and sometimes they would forego eating altogether and head straight to his bedroom.

Maggie was afraid she was becoming addicted to his touch. Just thinking about what they had done the previous night, in his kitchen, caused a smile to curve her lips. He was nothing if not inventive, and with the energy she'd been expending in the sack, it was no wonder she was famished all the time.

"Ah," Carly said in a knowing tone. "I'm right. He *is* your pilot."

Maggie's smile widened, but she only shrugged. "For now."

"For keeps, if you'd just stay."

Maggie gave Carly a warning look, but couldn't bring herself to dash the other woman's enthusiasm over what she was sure was a match made in heaven. "We'll see," she finally said. "I'm not committing to anything."

But as she turned back to the storeroom, she could have sworn she heard Carly mutter, "And therein lies the problem."

Was it true? She acknowledged that she was leery of getting involved with guys in uniform, but did she really have a problem making commitments? She thought of her last few relationships. The two boyfriends she'd had in Chicago had been decent guys—honest, caring and hardworking. They'd been funny, had made her laugh and she'd genuinely cared about them, but when they'd pushed for something more, she'd panicked. Not outwardly, of course, but their insistence on making the relationship permanent had usually marked the beginning of the end.

So far, Jack had kept his word and hadn't brought up Chicago, or asked her to reconsider staying on Whidbey Island. But he was quickly making it impossible for her to think of a future without him in it. He had all the qualities she'd ever wanted in a guy, and more.

Except, of course, for the damned uniform.

She would have given anything to have a crystal ball; to gaze into the future and be able to see if he would be there in ten or twenty years, or if, like her father and Phillip, he would simply vanish from her life. Did she have the courage to take that chance? Was she strong enough to survive another heartbreak? Losing Phillip had been hard, but hindsight at least gave her the realization that she'd been too young to get married. Even if things had worked out for them, they'd probably have ended up divorced, and where would she be now? Stuck on Whidbey Island, probably living with her brother and raising a couple of kids by herself. Just like her own mother had done.

With a sigh, she snatched up her backpack and sweater and walked back into the shop. "I have a headache," she fibbed to Carly in way of explanation. It wasn't far from the truth. Thinking about Phillip always made her head hurt. "Do you mind closing up?"

"Not at all, hon," Carly said, her face registering sympathy. "Go home and get some sleep—alone. You look like you could use it. I'll see you tomorrow. We'll get the tent set up then, okay?"

Maggie nodded. "That sounds great. See you tomorrow."

Her car was parked in the private space behind the shop, but Maggie decided she could use the fresh air to clear her head. Maybe the walk home would give her some focus and make her feel better. She hated that whenever she thought about Phillip her mood turned morose. She'd thought that after ten years she would be over him, but it seemed not a day went by when her thoughts didn't turn to him, even if it was only for an instant. She hated that.

For months after she'd moved to Chicago, she'd found herself looking for him, even though the rational part of her brain told her there was no reason on earth for him to come to Chicago. He certainly wouldn't come for her, and there were no navy installations in the city. Sometimes she would see a car identical to his and her heart would stop, only to realize it wasn't him. Those episodes had gradually diminished over time, but even now she'd occasionally find herself thinking about him without even realizing her thoughts had strayed there.

The worst part was that she could barely remember what Phillip looked like anymore, only the way he had made her feel. Had she truly loved him? She believed so, but then she'd believed he'd loved her in return, and that hadn't been the case. The result was that she no longer trusted her own feelings, never mind anyone else's. Her mother had suggested she go see someone, but at nineteen, she'd preferred to wallow in her own self-pity than to seek help.

As she walked past the shops and restaurants on Front Street, she drew in deep breaths of salty air. The fish pier thronged with people on this balmy afternoon, and the sidewalks were filled with families window-shopping, or stopping to enjoy an ice-cream cone or a slushy. A breeze lifted her hair from her neck, and Maggie watched a seagull wheel over the waters of Penn Cove, before floating on a current of air. She passed a rustic staircase that led down to the beach, and looked to see three children trying to skip stones across the water, while their mothers stood nearby, chatting and laughing.

She had missed this, she realized. She missed the small-town feel of Coupeville and the neighboring en-clave of Rocks Village, and the way the population changed during the summer months with the arrival of the tourists. She missed the ocean and the tang of salty air, and she missed the wide open vistas of water and mountains converging on the horizon. Most of all, she missed her family, and the sense that she belonged somewhere.

For the first time in ten years, she found herself con-sidering the possibility of returning to Whidbey Island, at least on a trial basis. She wasn't quite ready to com-mit to a permanent move, but her being a photographer at least gave her the freedom to move around. She didn't employ anyone, and she worked out of her own apartment, so she didn't even have the hassle of an office that she would need to sublet.

She told herself that her newfound perspective had nothing to do with the fact that Jack was building a house on the northern end of the island, or that his long-term plans included leaving the military and pursuing a career as a charter pilot. When she'd left Whidbey Island ten years earlier, she'd been emotionally compromised, and had not only condemned Phillip Woodman for ruining her life, but also transferred all those negative feelings to the island itself. She'd made Whidbey Island out in her mind to be the worst place imaginable; a veritable prison of sand and sea, but now that she was back, she realized she'd been wrong. Life here wasn't horrible by any stretch of the imagination, just different from Chicago.

Simpler. Easier.

She didn't know if she could be happy in the Pacific Northwest for the long haul, but the fact that Jack Callahan was here to stay made the option of extending her visit infinitely more appealing. Besides, before she'd gotten involved with wedding photography, her first love had been nature and wildlife photography, and Whidbey Island had that in abundance. With a smile, she lifted her face toward the sun and headed home.

THE FLYING CONDITIONS had been exceptional, with a high ceiling and visibility that extended for almost fifteen miles. Although restricted to airspace at the northern end of Whidbey Island and out over the open ocean, Jack had easily picked out the tiny community of Rocks Village from the air. He'd have liked to fly directly over the village, as he'd done over the town of Coupeville earlier in the week, but his flight plan didn't allow for any deviations, and the resultant complaints from the community wouldn't make it worthwhile. Still, he wondered what Maggie was doing as he rocketed through the skies overhead. Had she heard his engines? Had she thought of him?

He wasn't the kind of guy who used his position as a fighter pilot to attract women, but there was a part of him that wished Maggie could see him in the cockpit of the Growler, doing what he loved best. Well, he acknowledged ruefully, as he approached the airstrip and lined his aircraft up, he'd loved flying more than anything until he'd met Maggie. Given the choice of flying or making love to her, he'd have to choose her.

Every time.

Now, as he landed the jet and taxied to the hangar where the other jets were parked, he couldn't wait to call it a day and get home. As he raised the canopy and released his harness, his navigator and copilot, Will Robinson, did the same from the seat directly behind him, standing up and slapping the back of Jack's helmet.

"Nice flying, Callahan," Will remarked, swinging his legs over the side of the cockpit to climb nimbly to the tarmac. "Seems like longer than three weeks since we've done this."

Jack agreed, glad that his friend had finally arrived at Whidbey. He and Will, otherwise known as "Robot," had been flying together for almost six years, and there wasn't another navigator he'd trust more than his friend. He completed his engine shutdown procedures, then hoisted himself out of the narrow confines of the cockpit. He returned the salutes of the maintenance crew waiting to refuel and inspect the aircraft and fell into step beside Will.

He pulled his helmet off as they made their way over to flight ops for a quick debrief, already thinking about a shower and Maggie. Or better yet, a shower with Maggie. In thirty minutes, he'd be done for the day, and he couldn't wait to get back to the cottage. Maybe he'd invite Maggie out to see the plot of land where he planned to build a house. Despite knowing she didn't want to stay on the island, he knew she'd like the location, and he hadn't been kidding when he'd said he wanted her artistic opinion on how to situate the house on the land. The property was thick with pine trees, and he wanted to maintain as much of the natural landscape as possible, while capitalizing on the stunning views.

"Hey," Will said, "a bunch of the guys are grilling out tonight at McIsaac's place. Wanna join us?"

"Sounds fun," Jack said, "but I'm going to pass."

"Ah, plans with the lady friend?"

Jack grinned. "You bet."

"I still want to know how you manage to show up less than two weeks ago, and already you're hooking up with some babe."

Jack shrugged. No way was he going to share anything about Maggie with the guys in the squadron. He could take their good-natured ribbing, but he didn't think they'd understand that Maggie was so much more than just a hook up. "I don't know, man," he responded. "I met her the first night I got here, and we just clicked."

"Uh-huh." Will sounded unconvinced. "How many other guys did she click with before you showed up, huh?" The comment was made in jest, but Jack felt himself bristle.

"Maggie arrived on Whidbey Island the same night that I did, so there were no other guys, okay? She's a decent person, and I wish you wouldn't talk about her like that."

Will raised both hands in surrender. "Hey, man, no offense meant. I don't even know her. I'm sure she's great."

"Who's great?"

Both Jack and Will looked over as a third pilot joined them. Commander Ben Craig was a couple of years older and a full rank higher than both Jack and Will, and was considered to be the best pilot in the squadron, having completed more than one hundred sorties over Iraq and Afghanistan.

"Sir, we were just talking about Callahan's new love interest."

"Oh, yeah?" He peered over at Jack. "You work fast. She a local girl? Maybe my wife knows her."

"Yes, sir," Jack replied. "She grew up on Whidbey Island, but she left about ten years ago and moved to Chicago. She's just here for a couple of weeks to help run the family business."

"In other words, the perfect girlfriend, huh? In a couple of weeks she'll leave and you'll be a free man."

"No, sir," Jack insisted. "I'm doing everything I can to persuade her to stay."

"What's her name?"

"Maggie Copeland," he said reluctantly. "Her family owns a shop in Coupeville called Village Sea Glass. They sell sea-glass jewelry and some other glass stuff."

"Oh, I know the place," the commander said with a grin. "My wife grew up here, too, and she's pretty good friends with Eric Copeland."

They had almost reached the ops shack, and for a reason he couldn't decipher, the knowledge that the commander actually knew the Copeland family made him feel anxious. "Yeah, he's a good guy. I met him when I came out here a few months ago on a house-hunting trip. I'm actually renting a small cottage on the Copeland property."

"No shit. I remember my wife telling me a story about his sister. They're twins, right?"

Jack nodded, wishing he could prevent the other man from finishing his thought, but there was no way he could do that without appearing rude.

"Yeah, I remember," mused the commander. "She was engaged to a pilot. Then, just before the wedding, he up and married an admiral's daughter and left the Copeland girl in the lurch. What a guy, right?"

Will made a sound of disgust. "That's bullshit, man. I don't care if the chick he married *was* the admiral, that's no way to treat anyone." He slapped a hand to Jack's shoulder. "Although, lucky for you she *didn't* marry the bastard, right?"

Jack gave his friend a lukewarm smile. "Yeah. Lucky for me."

His chest ached for Maggie now that he understood what her issues were. No wonder she'd tried to keep him at a distance. She hadn't just been hurt by some random guy; she'd been betrayed and publicly humiliated by a pilot. Worse, the bastard had opted to marry a woman who had a powerful father, a guy who undoubtedly could impact his career progression. There was a part of Jack that wanted to hunt the prick down and beat the living crap out of him.

He realized now that he definitely had his work cut out for him in gaining Maggie's trust. He might have succeeded in claiming her body, but in light of what he now knew, he wondered if he had any chance in hell of claiming her heart.

<u>*11*</u>

MAGGIE SPENT A good part of the day working on items for the arts-and-crafts festival. The pictures of the orca whale had come out so well that she'd reprinted a bunch of copies using different finishing techniques, and had spent most of the day matting and framing the completed pieces. By the time she'd finished, it was early evening and she had almost two dozen photos ready for the fair. Her back ached from the long hours spent leaning over her work, and now she pressed a hand to her spine, wondering if a hot shower might relieve the discomfort.

Climbing the stairs, she stood in the doorway to her bedroom, remembering Jack's comment about feeling like a pervert. Now she surveyed the room through critical eyes. Why her mother or brother had never done anything to change the décor since she'd left home was beyond her. The room was like a time capsule to her early teen years, which was the last time she and her mother had redecorated. An enormous poster of Ricky Martin dominated one wall, with another of Britney Spears over her dresser and a full-length poster of the cast of *The Matrix* was on the backside of the bedroom door.

Maggie thought the room would make an ideal nursery. Walking to the end of the hallway, she pushed open the door of the bedroom where Danielle intended to put the babies. As bedrooms went, it was nicely situated, overlooking the front of the house, but to Maggie's mind, it was too far away from Danielle and Eric's bedroom.

She was still contemplating whether or not she had the guts to swap out the rooms, when her cell phone began to vibrate in her pocket. Pulling the device out, she saw it was Eric.

"Hey," she answered. "Having a great time?"

"Listen, sis, something's happened."

His voice was so somber that Maggie's heart lurched hard in her chest. Fear gripped her, and she reached out to hold on to the door frame. "What is it? Is Danielle okay? Are the babies okay?"

"Yes, everyone's fine. At least, they are now. Danielle started to go into early labor last night. By the time we got to the hospital, she was five centimeters dilated. They've stabilized her, and the contractions have stopped. She's resting now."

"Oh, my God." Danielle was only twenty-four weeks pregnant. Maggie wasn't a doctor, but even she could do the math, and delivering the twins so early could be extremely dangerous. Maggie didn't know what their chances might be if they were born so prematurely, but she knew they weren't great. "What happens now? Can they keep her going for another month or two?"

She heard Eric sigh on the other end and could picture him running his hands through his hair, making it stand on end. She could hear an intercom in the background, and realized he must be calling her from the hospital.

"Do you want me to come down there?" she asked.

"No, no," Eric said quickly. "There's nothing you can do, and Danielle's parents are here. Mom is flying in later tonight."

That didn't surprise Maggie. Valerie had always been there for her kids, and she'd be there now for Eric and Danielle. "That's good," she said. "So what happens now?"

"Well, it looks like we're going to extend our stay by at least another two months, or until the twins are born. The doctors won't let Danielle travel, and the only way to prolong the pregnancy is to keep her on absolute bed rest. At least we can stay with her parents, who've been terrific." There was silence as Maggie digested this information. "Maggie?"

"Yes, I'm here."

"Listen, I'm not asking you to stay until we get home. I know you have your own life in Chicago to get back to. But right after the festival ends, Carly was planning on driving down to Portland to spend some time with her mother, who isn't well. I won't ask her to change her plans, but I'll need to make some phone calls to see if I can get someone in to run the shop while she's gone."

"Eric, I'll stay." Maggie blurted out the words before she could change her mind.

"What?" She could hear the disbelief in her brother's voice.

"I said I'll stay. I'll watch the house and the shop, and I don't want you to worry about anything, okay?

Just take care of Danielle and those precious babies. Nothing else matters."

"Maggie, I don't know what to say."

She could hear the emotion in his voice and knew he was close to losing it. She couldn't imagine the fear and stress of what he must be going through, and the last thing she wanted was to add to that worry.

"Hey, it's okay," she assured him. "Besides, I have Jack to lend a hand if I need anything." Like a mind-blowing orgasm, for starters, although she certainly wouldn't share that detail with her brother.

"He's there already?" Eric's voice betrayed his shock. "But he's not due for at least another week."

"Yes, well, he showed up the day after you left."

"Jesus, Maggie, why didn't you call me to let me know? I feel terrible. I didn't even clean the cottage!"

"It's fine, Eric, don't worry. Apparently, he got released early from his last assignment and drove straight out to Whidbey Island. But he's settled in, the place is clean and cozy and he seems very happy there."

"That's great," Eric said with obvious relief. "He seems like a genuinely good guy, so I'd hate to let him down as a landlord."

Maggie smiled. "I think I can safely say he's more than satisfied with the services of his de facto landlady."

There was a shocked silence, and then Eric laughed softly. "You always manage to surprise me, Maggie. I'm not going to ask, because I'm not sure I want to know, but just…be careful, okay? I don't want to see you get hurt."

Again. He didn't say the word, but it hung there in the air between them.

"It's okay," Maggie said. "For the first time, I have my eyes wide open."

They spent the last few minutes of the conversation talking about the festival preparations and the shop before Eric hung up, promising to call again in a day or so.

Maggie turned the cell phone over thoughtfully in her hands. She tried to imagine what it would be like for Danielle to be confined to her bed for the next couple of months. She determined that the first thing she'd do would be to send her some jewelry-making supplies, which would at least keep her occupied. Then she'd move her bedroom to the end of the hallway, and redo her old bedroom as the nursery, which would bring the infants closer to their parents. She needed to stay positive, and decorating the nursery would help her believe that the babies would be okay. Feeling good about her decision, she closed the door and made her way slowly downstairs.

She'd actually agreed to stay in Rocks Village until Danielle and the babies were ready to come home. Realistically, that could be another eight to ten weeks. She thought of her small apartment in Chicago. She'd need to make arrangements for her mail to be forwarded, and she'd have to cancel her upcoming photo shoots, and recommend other professionals who might be willing to take on those projects. But she could do it. She *would* do it.

Oddly enough, the thought of shifting her entire life from Chicago to Whidbey Island didn't freak her out. Instead, she felt curiously at peace with her decision, and she realized it was because she'd already made up her mind to stay.

An hour later, having showered and feeling refreshed, she stood at the kitchen counter, making a list of all the things she needed to do if she was going to remain on Whidbey Island, whether it was for two more weeks, two more months or forever. The sheer number of details was daunting, and she'd need to make at least one trip back to Chicago to arrange for the shipment of her furniture. Most importantly, she needed to find a place to live here. She had no interest in living with Eric and Danielle, although they would probably try to change her mind. Neither did she want to live in the cottage, even if it was vacant. If she was going to do this, she needed to be completely independent and have her own apartment or house. Which meant she was going to need some steady income.

Maggie shifted her attention to her collection of newly framed photos, spread out on the long kitchen table, and considered them thoughtfully. If she was serious about staying, she would need to get her professional photography business up and running here on the island.

She had so much work to do, but she felt energized and ready for the challenge. The sound of a car drew her attention, and she watched through the window as Jack drove past the house and parked beside the cottage. He got out, still in his flight suit and carrying his gear in a duffel bag. Even from a distance, he looked mouth-wateringly handsome, and Maggie gave an appreciative sigh as she leaned her elbows on the counter and watched him. She thought he seemed preoccupied, but as he unlocked the door to the cottage, he paused and looked toward the main house. She debated on going out onto the porch to say hello, but he stepped into the cottage and closed the door behind him.

In the four days since their encounter in the dark room, she'd spent every night at the cottage. They had fallen into a routine, of sorts, and if she were to continue that routine, she would go down and knock on his door and he would invite her in. But there had been something about his manner tonight that gave her pause and made her reluctant to intrude on his privacy.

Since moving into the cottage, he'd been on what he called light duty, partly because he wasn't scheduled to arrive for at least another week, and because his copilot had only just arrived. But starting today, he would begin a full regimen of duties. She had a good idea what that meant, and knew he was likely worn out.

As hard as it would be, she wouldn't visit Jack tonight, and would instead concentrate on getting her own life back on track. With that thought in mind, Maggie gathered her papers together. She went into Eric's study, where she opened his laptop and began researching the current photographers on the island. If she was going to do this, she needed to know what she was up against for competition. There were more than a dozen photography businesses, nearly all of them located in Oak Harbor, but none in Coupeville or Rocks Village.

Maggie began adding more items to her growing list of things to do. When a sharp knock came at the back door, she was so engrossed in what she was doing that she startled. Rising to her feet, she smoothed a hand over her hair, knowing it had to be Jack. She was surprised to see the sun had set, and as she walked through the house, she flipped on lights. When she finally opened the back door, Jack stood there wearing a black, button-down shirt and a pair of dark jeans. He smiled when he saw her, but Maggie thought his eyes looked somber.

"Hi," she said, feeling unaccountably shy beneath his serious regard. "I wasn't expecting you."

He braced one arm against the door frame and leaned in toward her, looking impossibly sexy. "I don't know why not. I was expecting you to come down to the cottage, and when you didn't show up, and the house looked dark, I thought I should come check on you. Everything okay?"

"Of course."

He tipped his head. "Then why didn't you come down?"

Maggie bit her lip. "Because I knew you worked a full day at the base today, and you looked a little beat when I saw you come home tonight. I actually have a lot of work to do, so I thought I'd give you some space."

He straightened, his expression unreadable. "Maggie, I don't *need* space." Reaching out, he caught her by the upper arms. "I need *you*."

Maggie flushed beneath the intensity of his stare. "I'm sorry. I didn't want to be pushy. I was just trying to be considerate."

Jack framed her jaw in his big hands, and it was all Maggie could do not to turn her face into his palm. He looked so handsome and strong and decent that she wanted to curl herself into his masculine frame and just let him take care of her, the way he seemed to want to.

Jack dipped his head to look directly into her eyes. "Well, don't. If you decide not to come down to the cottage, you can bet I'm coming to you. Got it?"

Maggie nodded, pleasure unfurling deep inside her and slowly finding its way to every part of her body. "Got it."

"Good. Have you eaten?"

"No."

"Grab a sweater. I'm taking you out. There's a great little pub on the way to Oak Harbor that seems pretty popular. Interested?"

Maggie put a hand self-consciously to her hair. "Can you give me ten minutes?"

"You look great," he assured her, tugging a loose tendril of hair from behind her ear. "But take whatever time you need."

In the end, Maggie was ready to go in less than five minutes, half afraid Jack might change his mind if she dallied. She pinned her hair up at the back of her head with a large plastic clip, and decided her white jeans and turquoise T-shirt would have to do.

As they drove to Oak Harbor, Jack switched the radio to an upbeat station, reached across the center console and laced his fingers with Maggie's.

"How was your day?" he asked, glancing at her.

"I had a call from Eric," she said. "His wife is having problems with her pregnancy, and the doctors won't let her travel until after the twins are born."

He snapped his attention to her. "What does that mean for you?"

She tried to keep her tone light, not sure how he would feel about the news that she could be on Whidbey Island for another two months or so, and still not wanting to appear pushy. She certainly wouldn't tell him that she was considering relocating to the island on a more permanent basis.

"You met Carly, who works in the shop with Eric," she began. "She's leaving for Portland right after the arts-and-crafts festival, which means Eric doesn't have anyone to run the shop for him. He didn't ask me to stay, but I offered."

"For two months?" Jack's tone betrayed his astonishment.

"For however long he needs me."

She wasn't ready to tell Jack that she'd decided to

stay on Whidbey Island even after Eric returned with his family. Her insides were churning with emotions, and although Jack was a huge reason why she wasn't returning to Chicago, she didn't want to give him that power. She'd changed the course of her life once for a guy, and she wasn't quite ready to do it again.

Jack squeezed her hand, before raising it up to his lips and pressing a kiss against her fingers. "I'm sorry Danielle is having problems, but I'm glad you're staying, Mags."

"Me, too," Maggie said softly. "Although Eric was pretty surprised when I told him you'd already arrived. He didn't think you were coming for at least another week or two."

"What did you tell him?"

"Only that you seemed satisfied with the services of your de facto landlady."

Jack slid her a disgruntled look. "Well, not completely satisfied."

Maggie arched an eyebrow. "Oh, no?"

"Nope. If I was completely satisfied, you and I would have already spent a couple of hours at my cottage, and then headed out for dinner."

"Maybe we can save that for dessert," Maggie suggested.

Even by the dim lights of the dashboard, she could see his eyes grow heated, but was unprepared when he wrenched the wheel hard and pulled the big SUV to the side of the road in a spray of gravel and dirt. Outside of Maggie's window, the wooded embankment fell steeply away, and through the trees she could just make out the glittering waters of Penn Cove. Unfastening his seat belt, Jack leaned across the center console, keeping his eyes on Maggie's face as his fingers released her restraint.

"I've been trying to behave myself," he admitted with a wry smile, "but I decided to hell with it. I don't want to drive another mile without tasting you."

Maggie's breath hitched as he slid a hand to the nape of her neck and slowly drew her toward him. She fastened her gaze on his mouth. "I always was a dessert-before-dinner kind of girl," she murmured softly, and felt him smile against her mouth, just before he kissed her.

THE RESTAURANT, appropriately called Flyers, was doing a brisk business as they pulled into the parking lot. Jack found a space and then turned off the engine, turning to look at Maggie. He'd pulled her hair down from the clip and now it tumbled softly around her face and shoulders. He noted with satisfaction that she still looked a little disoriented from when he'd kissed her and her mouth was swollen and red.

He hadn't been able to help himself. She'd looked so distracted and disheveled when she'd answered the door, and when her appearance was combined with the dark house and the fact that she hadn't come to see him, he'd momentarily wondered if he'd interrupted something he'd rather not know about. In the next instant, he'd realized she'd been so engrossed in her task that she'd completely lost track of time. She'd had the look of someone who had just wakened from a dream.

He'd wanted to take her to bed right then and there. Commander Craig's words were still fresh in his head, and he'd had an almost overwhelming need to show Maggie that he wasn't like that other guy—the one who'd ditched her. He'd felt fiercely protective of her and oddly possessive, in a way he'd never felt about any woman before. He'd been able to keep his raging need for her subdued until she'd made the comment about dessert, and he knew he had to finally kiss her. There was no way he'd have been able to sit through a meal and be sociable without first slaking his need for her.

The kiss had quickly turned molten, and she hadn't protested when he'd pushed her shirt up and her bra down, and had kissed and sucked her breasts. If she hadn't brought him to his senses, he might have taken her, right there in the vehicle. But the oncoming head-lights of another car had made her push him away. Even then, he'd considered turning around, heading back to the cottage and not leaving for a week.

"Hey, you okay?" he asked, reaching over to run a knuckle along her cheek.

"Yes." She gave him a meaningful look. "But that really wasn't fair. Now I'll only be able to think about one thing while I'm in that restaurant."

"Oh, yeah? What's that?"

"You. Naked."

With a soft groan, Jack leaned toward her again, his body responding instantly. To his dismay, she laughed and put both hands against his shoulders, pushing him back.

"Oh, no, you don't," she said, smiling. "You already had part of your dessert before dinner. You're going to have to wait for the rest, if you haven't already ruined your appetite."

"Are you kidding? I don't think I'll ever get enough." Seeing the determination in her expression, he eased back and held up both hands in surrender. "Fine. Let's go, although I'm sorry now that I ever suggested we go out. When I think what we could be doing instead…"

Inside the restaurant, the atmosphere was noisy and crowded, and Jack immediately recognized several guys from his squadron. He pulled Maggie close with one arm around her shoulders.

"Do you want to have a quiet meal, just the two of us, or go join some of the guys from the base?" He had to bend his head to her ear and raise his voice to be heard, and Maggie gave him a tolerant look.

"I don't think there is any such thing as a quiet meal here tonight," she replied. "Besides, it looks like we might have to wait for a table. Why don't you put our name in, and we can join your friends until a table frees up?"

Jack nodded, and when he had given his name to the hostess, they carefully threaded their way through the crowded bar area to where several men had a table in the corner. It was moderately quieter there, and they greeted Jack with good-natured ribbing and raised fist-bumps.

"Hey, everyone," Jack said, pulling Maggie forward. "I'd like you to meet Maggie Copeland."

Jack sensed how uncomfortable Maggie was, but she smiled as they raised their glasses in greeting or reached out to shake her hand.

"Here," he said, dragging a free stool up to the edge of the table. "Have a seat. I'm going to get us a couple of drinks, but I'll be right back."

She swiveled to look up at him, and he could see the anxiety in her eyes at the thought of being left alone with the other men. "Can't I come with you?"

"I'll only be a minute," he said, squeezing her shoulders. "You'll be fine."

But he sensed how her gaze clung briefly to him as he headed toward the bar. Once he'd ordered drinks for both of them, he turned and watched her from a distance. The guys had engaged her in conversation, and if she really was nervous, she did a great job hiding it. That was just part of the reason he liked her so much. He got the sense that during her life, she'd done a lot of jumping without looking first. Most of the time, she'd landed on her feet. But a couple of times, like when she'd gotten engaged, she'd ended up getting hurt.

Her spontaneity was just one of the things he admired about her, and he intended that the next time she leaped, he'd be there to catch her. He was fiercely glad she'd agreed to stay in Rocks Village until Eric and Danielle came home. While they hadn't talked much about their future, Jack was more certain with each passing day that Maggie was the one for him. Being out in public together made him feel as if they were a real couple, and the fact that he'd introduced her to his buddies only solidified the feeling.

By the time he returned to the table, Maggie seemed more relaxed, and he knew the guys had gone to extra lengths to make her feel comfortable. He appreciated the gesture, but just in case any of them had the wrong idea, he handed Maggie her glass of wine, and then leaned in to plant a kiss on her mouth. When he pulled away, warm color rode high in her cheeks, and she rolled her lips inward, as if savoring the taste of him.

"Maggie told us she's into photography," said Mitch Lawrence, a young pilot whose duties also included being the public affairs officer for the base.

"That's right," Jack said, leaning his forearms on the table and bumping shoulders with Maggie. "You should see some of her work. It's pretty impressive."

"We have an opening for a reporter in our public affairs office," Mitch continued. "The job is a civilian position, and involves writing news and feature stories for our monthly magazine, as well as taking photos. If you're interested, I can set something up."

"Like an interview?" Maggie asked.

Mitch shrugged. "Why not?"

Jack looked over at Maggie, trying to read her expression, but she smiled and shook her head. "Thanks, but I'm not much of a writer. I can handle photography, but I'd be hopeless at writing news stories."

The conversation turned toward the different places each of them had been assigned over their time with the navy, and although Maggie didn't contribute much in the way of conversation, Jack watched as she followed the discussion. He loved watching her; she had one of the most expressive faces he'd ever seen, and everything she felt was right there in her eyes. As if sensing his perusal, she glanced over at him, and their eyes locked. Slowly, she smiled at him, and something tightened painfully in Jack's chest. He knew then that he was totally and completely head over heels for this woman.

At that moment, the hostess approached them, indicating their table was ready. Jack scooped up their drinks and after saying good-night to the others, followed Maggie through the bar area and into the restaurant. As they approached their table, Jack became aware of a couple sitting near the windows. They were probably Jack's age, and based on the man's haircut and bearing, Jack guessed he was in the military. He probably wouldn't have given them a second look, except that the man was staring at Maggie. He couldn't blame the guy for looking—Maggie was a beautiful woman—but where most men would have looked away by now, this one continued to watch her.

Deliberately seating Maggie with her back to the couple, Jack held out her chair for her. As he did, the man stood up and came over to their table. Every cell in Jack's body was on high alert, yet the man seemed almost hesitant to intrude.

"Excuse me," he said to Jack, but his attention was on Maggie.

Maggie looked up expectantly, but there was no recognition in her eyes, only polite interest. Jack felt himself relax fractionally. As crazy as it seemed, for one instant, he'd wondered if the guy was her ex-fiancé. Now the man shifted his weight and laughed a little uncomfortably.

"I'm sorry to bother you, but you look so familiar to me." He focused on Maggie. "Are you—are you Maggie Copeland?"

Maggie's smile widened, but her expression was a little bemused. "Yes, I am. Do I know you?"

"I'm sure you don't remember me. It's been a long time. I actually feel like an ass even intruding on your evening, but I couldn't believe it was really you." He extended his hand to her. "I'm Nathan Stone. I used to be stationed at the air base."

Jack watched as the color drained out of Maggie's face. "Yes," she said, her voice so low he almost didn't hear her. "I remember you."

Jack had seen and heard enough. He didn't know who Nathan Stone was, but he could see his presence was upsetting to Maggie. He stepped forward. "I'm Jack Callahan. It's great that you recognize Maggie, but we're just trying to have a quiet dinner." He looked meaningfully toward the man's table, where his wife or girlfriend still sat, watching them curiously. "And I think your date is waiting for you."

Looking back at his table, the man raised one finger to the woman, then returned his attention back to

Maggie. "You look good—really good. I'm glad. I just wanted to say that I didn't know anything about what was happening back then, okay? He was my best friend, but I never knew about—about that other thing. I just want you to know that."

Maggie nodded and swallowed hard. "Thank you. I appreciate that."

"Okay, good." The man shifted uncomfortably. "Well, I'll let you get back to your night. Sorry to disturb you."

He returned to his table, and Jack watched as he took the woman's hand across the table and leaned forward to talk softly to her. The woman's expression turned to one of sympathy, and she glanced over at Maggie.

"Hey," Jack said, stroking his fingers along the back of her hand. "Let's just get out of here."

She gave him a grateful smile, but Jack didn't miss the sheen in her eyes, which she quickly blinked away. "That sounds good," she said, nodding. "I'm not really that hungry, anyway."

Jack pulled her chair back, and because she seemed so vulnerable at that moment, he wrapped an arm around her shoulders and hugged her against his body as he led her out of the restaurant. He could feel her trembling, and his arm tightened protectively around her. When they reached his Land Rover, he handed her into the passenger seat and then leaned across her to buckle her in. But instead of closing the door, he braced one hand on the back of her seat and looked at her.

"Are you okay?"

"Yes, I'm fine. He just— I wasn't—" Breaking off abruptly, she made a groaning sound of frustration and rubbed her hands over her face before giving him a bright smile. "He was the last person I ever expected to see tonight."

Jack waited expectantly, but when she didn't say anything, he made an impatient gesture. "So who the hell was he?"

Maggie sighed. "He was supposed to be the best man at my wedding."

12

EVEN KNOWING THAT Maggie had once been engaged, the information rattled Jack. But instead of letting her see how he felt, he bracketed her face in his hands and stared into her eyes. "Okay, big deal. You're probably going to run into other people who knew you back then. I know seeing him threw you, but you handled yourself really well."

Maggie smiled, and turned her cheek into his hand. "It helped that you were there."

"Yeah, well, I'm glad I was."

"What if it had been *him?* Phillip Woodman?"

Jack hadn't known the name of her former fiancé, and it didn't mean anything to him now, but he realized he disliked hearing the bastard's name on her lips.

"You would have been fine. And I promise you, he would have taken one look at you and realized he made the biggest mistake in the world in letting you go."

Maggie smiled, and Jack could see she was relaxing. "Thank you, Jack. You're so sweet."

"I'm not sweet, Maggie. Right now, I feel anything but sweet." He glanced around the dark parking lot and back toward the entrance of the restaurant. "Are you still hungry?"

"Let's just go home."

She'd done it again, referring to Whidbey Island as home, and Jack felt a keen sense of satisfaction at her words. "Okay, sweetheart." Dipping his head, he pressed a warm kiss against her mouth. "But just for the record, I think the guy is a complete moron."

He wasn't sure who he referred to, her ex-fiancé for ditching her, or Nathan Stone for having the poor taste to come over and talk to her, knowing he would be dredging up bad feelings. He was biased against anyone who could make Maggie feel sad. Closing the passenger door, he walked around the vehicle, slid behind the wheel and thrust it into Drive, surprised when she reached over and put a hand on his thigh.

"Thank you."

Jack gave her a wink. "You bet."

They drove back to the house in silence, and Jack could see that Maggie was lost in her own thoughts, although she left her hand on his leg. Even through the denim of his jeans, he could feel the warmth of her fingers, and couldn't prevent his body from responding. He felt like a dick for thinking about sex at a time like this, but Maggie had had that effect on him since the first night he'd met her. But she seemed oblivious to his reaction to her. Hell, if she weren't actually touching him, he doubted she'd remember he was in the car with her. Even when they passed the spot where he had pulled over to kiss her, she didn't appear to notice. It wasn't until they reached the cottage that she roused herself and seemed to become aware of her surroundings.

"Would you rather be alone?" Jack asked quietly. He didn't want to let her return to the big house by herself, but she seemed so preoccupied that he wondered if she might not need some time to herself to sort things out. To his relief, she shook her head.

"No. I'd rather be with you. Unless *you'd* rather be alone…"

"Not a chance," he said quickly. "I don't have to be back at the base until the day after tomorrow, so I am all yours, sweetheart."

She let her gaze drift over him. "That sounds…promising."

Jack laughed, relieved that she wasn't going to let her encounter with Nathan Stone ruin her night. "Oh, yeah? What do you have in mind?"

"Why don't I show you?" she said suggestively, and ran her hand along his thigh to his crotch, where he was already half-erect and quickly responding to the promise in her voice.

He was out of the vehicle and opening her door almost before she could finish her sentence. But instead of letting her step out of the Land Rover, he unbuckled her restraint and hauled her into his arms, lifting her against his chest as she gave a cry of surprise and clutched at his shoulders.

"What are you doing?" she asked as he kicked the door shut and took the steps to the cottage two at a time.

"Making sure you don't change your mind," he growled, pushing the door open and striding through the dark house to his bedroom.

Setting her on her feet, he didn't give her time to step away, but dragged her up against his body and kissed her, hard and deep. He wanted to erase any thoughts of Phillip Woodman from her mind. He wanted to imprint himself on her so that she had no doubts about whom she was with. He'd make sure she never had any doubts about how completely desirable she was.

Maggie responded, winding her arms around his neck and pushing her fingers through his hair, rubbing her fingertips against his scalp. Jack slid his hands beneath the hem of her T-shirt, sliding his palms over the warm skin of her ribs and around to her back. His fingers explored the bumps of her spine and the gentle thrust of her shoulder blades, before he deftly unfastened the hooks on her bra, releasing the undergarment and freeing her breasts.

"Here," she said, and pulled away just long enough to drag the shirt over her head.

Jack pulled the bra free of her arms, then cupped both of her breasts in his hands, lifting them and pushing them together, admiring their plumpness. At the same time, Maggie's hands were busy working the fastening on his belt. Loosening the buckle, she quickly undid the button and opened his jeans, sliding her hand inside his boxers to curl her fingers around his length. Jack nearly groaned at the exquisite sensation.

"You're so hot," she gasped. "Take these off."

Releasing her luscious breasts, Jack bent and removed his shoes and then peeled his shirt off, dropping it onto the floor before he pushed both his jeans and his boxers down over his hips and kicked them free. Maggie was already removing her white pants, her eyes riveted on him in the darkness.

She started to reach for him, but Jack stepped quickly away before she could touch him, and switched on one of the bedside lamps, illuminating the room. He drew the shades over the windows, and then turned to look at Maggie.

She stood by the foot of the bed, and as soon as

he turned on the light, flattened her hands over her breasts in a gesture of modesty. She looked so incredibly sexy, that for a moment Jack just stood and gaped. Her waist was slender, but her hips and ass were lusciously curved. His eyes lingered on the narrow strip of dark curls at the juncture of her thighs. Dark red curls, which he knew were soft and springy to the touch. She could have been a pin-up girl from the forties. Her skin was pale and completely unblemished, without so much as a freckle anywhere. Behind her hands, he knew her nipples were large and pink tipped. He couldn't believe that she would hide them.

"Don't." Jack stepped around the bed and slowly pulled her hands away from her body. "You are so beautiful to me, Maggie. I don't want you to hide yourself from me, ever."

"Sorry." She gave a self-conscious laugh and pressed herself against him until her breasts were squashed against his chest. "It's just that I realized we've never had the lights on. Not once. We've always been in a dark bedroom—or in the darkroom. I didn't think I'd feel so…so exposed."

Jack slid his arms around her, his hands touching her everywhere, smoothing over her back and down over the silken curve of her buttocks. "Get used to it," he said in a husky voice. "I like being able to see you. All of you. You have the most expressive face, and I love watching you when you come."

"Oh," she sighed, and pressed her face against his neck, her mouth opening on his skin and alternately kissing and licking at his flesh. He could feel her mouth curve into a smile against his neck, and her heat and scent invaded his senses. He was fully erect, pressed against her hip, and she rubbed against him as she hugged him.

"Maggie," he groaned. "You're killing me."

"Oh, yeah?" Her voice was muffled. "What do you want me to do about it?"

"Put me out of my misery." His hands cupped her rear and lifted her against his throbbing dick to emphasize his meaning. "Please."

"Mmm, I'd be happy to," she whispered into his ear, and swirled her tongue around the edge until he shuddered lightly with sensation. Before he realized her intent, she stepped back and pushed firmly against his chest, until he sat down on the end of the bed. "Oh, wow," she murmured, her eyes dropping to where he was stiffly erect. Her playfulness abruptly ended, and she straddled his knees and reached down to curl her fingers around him.

"Oh, yeah," he said hoarsely. "That feels so good. Come here."

Grasping her hips, he drew her closer, until she had to bend one leg onto the mattress beside him or risk losing her balance. The movement opened her, and he slid a hand between her thighs to stroke her. She gasped softly and put a hand on his shoulder to steady herself. Her breathing quickened as he parted her slippery flesh and eased a finger inside her.

"Oh, man," he groaned, and withdrew his finger to swirl her moisture around and over her clitoris, before easing back inside her. Her fingers tightened around his cock, and she slid her fist over him, matching his movements. "Ah, babe, I need to be inside you."

Withdrawing his hand, he jerked her forward until she sat on his knees, with one foot on the floor, and one still bent on the bed. He stared at her for a long moment, his eyes drifting over her features until they lingered on her mouth. Then, burying one hand deep in her hair and fisting his fingers in the unruly mass, he pulled her face to his and covered her mouth with his lips. The kiss wasn't soft or gentle; it was hard and deep, and Maggie responded by curling her arms around his head and holding him in place, even as she shifted closer on his lap. Then, raising herself up, she positioned herself over his straining cock, and slowly eased herself down until he was seated deep inside her.

Jack grasped her ass in his hands and helped her lever herself over him, even as she deepened the kiss, spearing her tongue against his and making small, needy sounds in her throat. She rode him like that for several blissful minutes, until she broke away with a soft gasp.

"I'm so close," she panted.

"Here," Jack said, and lifted her away from him. "Let's try this." Standing up, he turned her toward the bed. "Lie down on the bed. On your stomach."

Maggie's expression turned hot, and she did as he asked, climbing onto the bed and laying on her stomach with her legs slightly parted. "Like this?" she asked, peering at him.

She looked like a decadent offering. "Raise your hips," he instructed, and grabbing a pillow, he bunched it beneath her. "Oh, yeah, just like that."

Standing behind her, he stroked her again and she moaned loudly and pushed back against his hand. "Oh," she breathed, "that feels so good."

Jack's own breathing was heavy, as he inserted first one finger into her slick heat, and then a second, thrusting gently as she arched her back and tried to get closer. Finally, when he could sense that she was getting close, he withdrew his hand and positioned himself at her entrance, with one hand on her hip. Surging forward, he buried himself inside her, the sensation of her body tightening around him so intensely that for a moment, he thought he'd lose it right there. He had to stop in order to regain control, but Maggie would have none of it, pushing herself back against him.

"Oh, please," she said, her voice breathless, "don't stop."

Knowing he was a complete goner, Jack bent forward until his chest brushed against her back, and his hips curved around her buttocks. He swept her hair over her shoulder and gently bit the curve her neck, scraping his teeth over her supple skin. Reaching beneath her, he stroked and fondled her breasts, before dipping lower, to where they were joined. Their position gave him unhindered access to her, and he stroked a finger hard across her swollen flesh, feeling her tighten around him as pleasure swept over her. Only when she cried out in release, and he felt her convulsing around him, did he finally let go, pouring himself into her with a hoarse shout of satisfaction. The force of his climax was so intense that his strength gave out, and he collapsed weakly on top of Maggie, crushing her feminine form into the mattress.

After a moment, Jack withdrew from her body and rolled to his back beside her, breathing heavily. Groping blindly with one hand, Maggie reached out and laced her fingers with his, squeezing tightly. Turning his head, he found her watching him through sleepy, satisfied eyes. Jack summoned enough energy to raise himself up on one elbow and stroke the damp hair back from her temple, before he turned her onto her side and curled his body around hers. She made a soft sound of approval and dragged his arm across her body. Jack sucked in a deep breath and tried to control his heart, which still pounded hard inside his chest. Reaching down, he grabbed a soft throw from the foot of the bed and pulled it over both of them, cocooning them in its warmth.

MAGGIE MUST HAVE fallen asleep, because when she opened her eyes again, she was beneath the covers with Jack's big body wrapped around her. Her head rested on his chest, and his hard thigh was wedged between hers. Through the drawn shades of his bedroom, she could just make out the pale glimmer of sunshine. She blinked slowly and stretched experimentally, aware that she was plastered against him from her chest to her ankles.

Jack mumbled something incoherent and shifted closer. Maggie might have tried to ease away, but her hair was caught beneath him, and there was no way she could disentangle herself without waking him. Instead, she lay still and listened to the steady thump of his heart beneath her ear, and slowly took stock of their positions. Her hand rested lightly on his ribs, and she became aware of the movement of his chest as he breathed, deeply and evenly. Heat poured off him, warming her, and his arm was a heavy weight across her waist.

The sheets smelled clean and crisp, but beneath that, she could smell the warm, musky scent of sex. She realized she had only to slide her hand lower to explore him. The knowledge caused a stirring low in her womb. Biting her lip, she glanced at Jack's face, but he didn't stir. His lashes were dark and lush against his chiseled cheekbones, and she found she missed the glittering caramel of his eyes when he was awake and watching her. Slowly, she eased her hand down over his abdomen, feeling the taut ridges of his muscles. When she encountered the light furring of hair that extended south from his navel, she followed it with her fingertips, feeling the springy curls around his penis.

His semi-erect penis.

Maggie's eyes flew to Jack's face, but he must have been having a nice dream, because he slept deeply, slack jawed and oblivious to her intimate explorations. She touched him, carefully stroking the soft flesh until it began to swell and harden beneath her hand. She was tempted to peek beneath the covers to see the impact she was having, but didn't want the cool air to wake him. She imagined ducking beneath the blankets and taking him in her mouth, tasting him and licking along his length. She wanted to feel him against her tongue, to draw on him the way she would a Popsicle.

Just thinking about doing those things to him caused something hot and needy to unfurl low in her womb. His leg was still wedged high between hers, and it was all she could do not to ride the big muscle of his thigh. Instead, she kept still except for the rhythmic stroking of her hand over his stiff erection. Slowly, she became aware that his breathing had changed, and his body had tensed. Glancing at his face, she saw him watching her through his lashes, his hazel eyes glittering hotly.

"Don't stop now," he said, his voice roughened with sleep and arousal. "Not when it seems the dream I was having is actually real."

Maggie let out a soft huff of laughter. "Oh, this is real, I promise," she said, rubbing her cheek against him as she continued to touch him, running a thumb over the wide head of his penis. When she encountered moisture, she felt an answering flood of liquid heat between her own thighs. Raising herself up on an elbow, she bent over Jack's prone body and pressed a moist kiss to the center of his chest, before slowly dragging her mouth to his nipple. He moaned as she flicked her tongue over the small nub, teasing him the way he enjoyed teasing her.

"Do you like that?" she asked, squeezing him beneath the covers.

"I'd like to wake up like this every morning," he assured her, and ran a hand over her shoulder and down her back.

"You feel so good," she said in awe, stroking him. "I've been thinking about all the things I'd like to do to you and getting pretty worked up."

"Really?" His voice sharpened with interest. "I can help you with that."

Before she realized his intent, he rolled on his side toward her, pushing her flat on her back and pulling both her legs over his hips, so that her bottom was pressed against his groin.

"Oh," Maggie breathed, understanding his intent. "This is...nice."

"You bet." He smiled. "This way, I can still hold you, and yet I have unimpeded access to everything."

He demonstrated by bending his head and kissing her, while simultaneously stroking her breasts and then moving his hand over her stomach and lower. Nudging her thighs open with his hand, he cupped his hand over her, caressing her. Then, shifting his hips, he was right there, easing himself into her. Whereas the previous night there had been an urgency to their lovemaking, and Maggie had been desperate to have him inside her, this morning was different.

Jack took his time kissing her, exploring her mouth in an almost leisurely manner, while he established a rhythm that was slow and languorous and drove Maggie wild.

"Don't rush it," he soothed, as if sensing her rising need. He skated his mouth along her jaw and caught her earlobe between his teeth, never stopping his maddening pace. "Just enjoy it. Let yourself go."

He punctuated his words with another long, lazy thrust of his hips, but this time he reached down and pressed his fingers against her, and Maggie came apart. Jack kissed her hard, capturing her muffled cries of pleasure. Her own release triggered his, and with one last, bone-melting thrust, he stiffened and Maggie could feel him surge inside her.

The lay entwined and breathless for several long minutes, until Jack withdrew himself from her body and disentangled himself from her limbs.

"Lady," he growled softly, bending over to plant another kiss on her mouth, "you are going to kill me."

Maggie smiled, feeling satisfied and ridiculously pleased with herself. She waited while Jack left the bedroom to clean up, then returned with a warm washcloth for her. She tried not to blush when he insisted on cleaning her himself, but it was impossible to be embarrassed around Jack. He was unabashedly comfortable with his own nudity, and he made no pretense of the fact that he preferred to have Maggie nude, too.

Now he climbed back into bed with her, bunched the pillows behind his broad shoulders and pulled Maggie up beside him. "How are you doing this morning?" he asked.

Maggie knew he referred to the incident from the previous night, when she'd admitted to being completely freaked out by running into Nathan Stone.

"I'm good," she assured him. "Part of the reason I

didn't want to come back here was because I knew I'd run into people who remembered what happened. I just didn't want to deal with it, but I guess you can't hide from your past forever."

"Nope," Jack agreed. "Better to accept it and move on."

"I'm trying." Maggie was silent for a moment. "What about you? No skeletons in your closet?"

Jack laughed softly. "Oh, sure. Everyone has skeletons."

Maggie couldn't imagine Jack having anything in his past that he might be ashamed of. "Tell me."

He shrugged and traced a lazy pattern on her arm with his fingers. "I told you my dad was gone a lot when I was a kid. His air-force career required that he move every few years, but after doing that a couple of times, my mom put her foot down. She didn't want to keep relocating, not with a kid. So she stayed in Colorado with me, and my dad continued with his career."

"Why didn't they just get divorced?"

"I don't know. He came home whenever he could, but I remember them sleeping in separate rooms." He shrugged. "I knew they were having problems, but I always thought they would work it out. I never expected them to get divorced."

"I'm sorry," Maggie murmured. "That must have been hard on you, only seeing your dad every once in a while."

"Well, not as hard as the time I came home early from school and found my mom in bed with the neighbor."

Maggie swiveled her head to look at him. His expression clearly reflected the remembered hurt and anger he had felt. "How old were you?"

"I was almost twelve. Our school had a water main break, so they sent everyone home early." He looked down at her. "The thing is, I really liked the guy she was with, but I was furious that she'd betrayed my dad. I was so pissed off at her that I called my dad and told him."

Maggie drew in her breath. "Oh, wow."

He gave a bitter laugh. "Yeah. That got him home in a hurry, but it was too late. They got divorced and I started spending my summers in Washington State."

"It wasn't your fault," Maggie said, because looking at his face, she could see that even after all this time, he blamed himself.

"Wasn't it? If I hadn't made that call…"

"They were already having problems," she reminded him.

He sucked in a breath and blew it out hard. "But I knew how my dad felt about infidelity. He had this thing about divorce, and how he'd never let it happen to him. Even though he and my mom weren't close, he believed that marriage was a forever commitment. He could have gone on the way they were indefinitely, I think."

"But your mother couldn't. She was lonely. She needed someone."

Jack gave a huff of bitter laughter. "But did it have to be our neighbor? And why couldn't she have had the decency to divorce my dad first before she got involved with another guy? I might have been able to forgive her, if that was the case."

Okay, so he definitely had issues with infidelity. Good to know, not that she'd ever give him any cause for concern. Any woman lucky enough to have Jack Callahan in her life should have her head examined if she so much as looked at another guy.

"Maybe, on some level, she knew that having an affair was the only way your dad would ever let her go," she ventured.

"Yeah, well, my phone call sure got the ball rolling."

Raising herself on one elbow, Maggie traced his mouth with her finger. "Think of it this way—if they hadn't gotten divorced, you might never have spent your summers on Whidbey Island."

"She sent me out here because she didn't want to leave me alone during the day, but I always wondered if it was because she wanted to be alone with *him*."

"So she and the neighbor never got married or anything?"

Jack shook his head. "No. When I was about fifteen, he moved away. I never saw him again."

"Are your parents still alive?"

"Yes. My mom still lives in Boulder, and my dad retired from the air force and lives in Texas now. I see him a couple of times a year. Actually, we have a pretty good relationship."

"And your mom?"

Jack shrugged. "I had a harder time forgiving her. Don't get me wrong, I love her a lot. But our relationship has always been a little distant."

Maggie stroked his arm, trying to imagine what it would be like to be married to a man who cared more about his career than he did his family. That had to have caused an enormous amount of hurt and resentment. In retrospect, maybe it was better that her own father hadn't stuck around. How much worse would it be knowing that your own father didn't love you enough to want to be with you? At least her dad had left before she and Eric had been born. When she was a little girl, Maggie's mother had often said that if he'd stayed long enough to actually meet Maggie and Eric, he never would have left, because he would have fallen instantly and completely in love with them.

"You're not very much like your dad," she said softly. "I mean, from what I can tell, you love your career, but I don't think you'd put it ahead of your family."

Jack looked at her in surprise. "You're right, I do love my career. There's nothing quite as exhilarating as flying, and the guys in my squadron are like family. But if I get married, my wife and kids will always come first, no question." He hesitated. "I made a promise to myself that if I ever had kids, they'd never have to wonder about my feelings for them, because I'd tell them every day. And I'd never cheat on my wife. If there's one thing I could never tolerate or forgive, it's infidelity."

"Ah, so maybe you are like your dad."

He turned to look at her. "I just think that if you've committed yourself to somebody, then you don't disrespect them by screwing around behind their back. I would never do that." Reaching out, he stroked a finger along Maggie's cheek. "When I give myself to someone, I do it completely. And I expect the same in return."

Maggie swallowed hard, feeling a lump forming in her throat. Not trusting herself to speak, she simply nodded and laced her fingers with his. He'd made it clear that he intended to remain on Whidbey Island. He was building a house. He had plans to run a charter flight business after he left the military. He had his life so perfectly mapped out, and Maggie was beginning to hope that there might be some room in that life for her.

13

THE DAY BEFORE the festival, Maggie found herself too busy to worry about anything except getting their tent ready for the opening day of the fair. She and Carly spent the morning arranging the items they would sell at the festival. They had hired a local girl to help them out with the sales, and while Maggie and Carly prepared the tent, she oversaw the shop. Meanwhile, hundreds of exhibitors poured into the tiny town of Coupeville, and the waterfront streets were soon lined with festive tents. Maggie had brought her collection of wildlife photos to the shop, and when Carly had first seen them, she'd been speechless.

"Maggie," she said, standing back to admire a photo, "you missed your calling. You're wasting your talents in wedding photography. You should always be doing nature or wildlife photos. Look at the colors you captured in that sunset! And I don't know how you achieved that particular effect with the whale—he seems to glow against the sky."

"I can't take all the credit," Maggie commented,

although the effusive praise was heartening. "I just worked with what nature provided."

"Oh, no," Carly protested. "You took what nature provided and brought it to the next level."

Maggie smiled, pleased in spite of herself. "I actually enjoy portrait photography. Especially the babies. I can't wait until Danielle and Eric have the twins. I plan on documenting every minute of their lives with my camera."

Carly made a disgruntled noise and arched one eyebrow. "That's going to be a little difficult to do from Chicago," she noted sourly.

"Well, that's just it. Since I told Eric I would stay here until after the twins are born, I thought I might as well come back for good. You know, find a place to live, hang my shingle and all that."

Carly gaped at her for a minute as if unable to comprehend what she was saying. "Are you serious?"

Maggie nodded. "I am. I'm going to try it, at least for a year, and if it doesn't work out then I'll reevaluate and decide what to do from there. But I could use the change, and I think Eric and Danielle could use an extra hand, at least for that first year."

Carly's expression turned sly. "And your decision doesn't have anything to do with a certain sexy pilot, does it?"

"It might," Maggie acknowledged with a smile. "But for now, I've only told him that I'm here until the twins come home." She shrugged. "I don't want him to think that the only reason I'm staying is because of him. That might freak him out."

"Or it might not. Did you think that he might be holding back a little because he knows that eventually you're going to return to Chicago? You should tell him that you've decided to stay."

Maggie made a sound of disagreement, recalling his views on commitment. He'd said that when he made a commitment to a woman, he did it completely. She knew that he was ready to commit himself to her. The knowledge both thrilled and terrified her. She didn't know if she was ready to reciprocate. Not yet. She was almost there, but taking that last step and telling him how she felt about him scared the hell out of her.

She hadn't seen Jack since the previous day, and she acknowledged that she missed him. He'd called in the early afternoon to say he was having dinner with his architect, and had invited her to join them, but she'd refused, not wanting to intrude on business. Despite having woken up at five-thirty, his Land Rover had already been gone, and she was feeling the effects of not having seen him for twenty-four hours. She'd slept poorly without him, and felt tired and cranky. The knowledge that she wouldn't see him tonight either only intensified her sour mood.

She just needed to get through the festival, and then she could begin making some solid decisions about her future.

About him.

As she and Carly put the finishing touches on the tent, she thought about how she would get her new photography business up and running. Thankfully, her brother knew just about everybody on the island, and he'd display her work in his shop. But she'd need to establish her own clientele, and maybe open a small studio on the island. The prospect was both unnerving and exciting.

As the late afternoon stretched into early evening,

Maggie stood on the main street and gaped at the transformation. Both sides of the street were lined with tents, and even though the fair didn't begin until the next day, small groups of people made their way down the center of the streets for an advance viewing of the items for sale. Soon, the police would herd them out of the festival area, and the waterfront would become off-limits until the morning. Food vendors had also set up their booths by the famous pier, and Maggie's mouth watered in anticipation of funnel cakes and cotton candy. The weather promised to cooperate, and Maggie found herself looking forward to the festival.

"I've never seen so many exhibitors before," observed Carly, who had come to stand beside her. "Tomorrow is going to be standing room only."

Maggie silently agreed. She hadn't attended the annual festival in over ten years, and the last time she had, there'd been half as many exhibitors as there were now. Suddenly, her gaze sharpened on a couple who slowly made their way down the center of the street. She frowned, and then quickly ducked back into the tent. She'd recognized Nathan Stone immediately, and he was with the same woman he'd been with at the restaurant.

"Are you okay?" Carly asked, stepping into the tent behind her.

"Yes. I just saw somebody that I'd rather avoid right now." Stepping past Carly, she jerked the flaps of the tent closed and began tying them securely. Through the opening, she could see Nathan and the woman coming closer. They looked relaxed and happy, and with a sense of relief, Maggie realized they hadn't seen her.

She tried to recall what she knew of Nathan. He'd been a pilot, too, and had been Phillip's closest friend.

Maggie hadn't known him well, as Phillip had tended not to introduce her to his friends very often, but what she knew of him, she'd liked. He'd always been kind to her. But no way did she want to get into any discussions with him, not when the only thing they had in common was Phillip. As they drew level with the tent, Maggie stepped back, out of sight.

"Who is that?" Carly asked, peering over her shoulder through the opening. "Why are you hiding?"

Maggie grimaced. "That's Nathan Stone. He was Phillip's best friend, and was supposed to stand up at our wedding."

"Ah." Carly put a sympathetic arm around Maggie's shoulder and gave her a squeeze. "You're bound to run into people who knew you from those days. You have nothing to be ashamed of."

Maggie nodded. "I know. But I keep thinking that if Nathan is still in the area, maybe Phillip is, too."

Curly looked curiously at Maggie. "You don't know where Phillip is living?"

"Of course not. Why would I? That's part of the reason I moved to Chicago, so I wouldn't ever have to worry about running into him. Or his wife. I assumed they'd stayed here on Whidbey Island until he was re-assigned somewhere else. But where that was, I have no idea." She snorted. "Maybe he got some cushy assignment in Washington, D.C."

Carly shrugged. "I don't know where he went, either, and trust me when I say that nobody who cares about you ever asked."

Maggie gave her a grateful smile. "Well, at least he reimbursed my mother for the cost of the caterer and the band."

Carly snorted. "That wasn't Phillip who did that—it was his new father-in-law."

The admiral.

For just a moment, Maggie allowed herself to recall the events of that day, when she'd learned that Phillip hadn't actually deployed for six months, as he'd told her. After his friend had dropped that bombshell, Maggie had fled the air base and returned home, nearly hysterical. When her mother had calmed her down long enough to get the story from her, Valerie's face had turned hard. Maggie could still see the fierceness of her mother's expression as she'd dragged her to the car. They'd driven to the base, and Valerie had refused to leave until she'd been allowed to speak to Phillip's commanding officer, who had confirmed that Phillip had never actually deployed aboard a carrier, but had, in fact, married an admiral's daughter.

That had been all Valerie Copeland had needed to hear. She hadn't asked for details, or even where Phillip was living. She'd simply packed Maggie back into the car and they'd driven home.

"That's it," she'd told Maggie in a no-nonsense voice. "It's over and that boy is out of your life. He's married, and that's not something that's going to change. So now you need to make some decisions. You can't stay here. Not with him living so close. He'll only drag you down and ruin your life. You need to get away."

Maggie had agreed. While she'd wanted to confront Phillip and demand an explanation, her mother had finally dissuaded her. What good would it do? Her heart would still be broken, her life still turned upside down. Better to walk away with her dignity intact. Valerie had hoped that Maggie would finally go to college, but Seattle hadn't been far enough away from Whidbey Island for Maggie. So she'd gone to Chicago, and she hadn't looked back.

JACK GLANCED SURREPTITIOUSLY at his watch, just wanting the briefing to end. He'd been through this drill so many times before that he could practically recite the rules from memory. His squadron had just been notified that they would depart the following day for a three-day sea exercise. While not uncommon, Jack had never before received so little advance notice. This was a readiness test, to determine their capability to respond in the event of an actual combat emergency. Even now, the carrier that they would report to was hundreds of miles out to sea, and Jack and his squadron would join them tomorrow and spend the next day practicing carrier takeoffs and recoveries.

He should be ecstatic. This was what he excelled at—what he loved to do. Instead, all he could think was that he didn't want to leave Maggie, even for three days. He had hoped he'd be able to spend some time with her at the festival. He knew she was exhibiting some of her work, and he wanted to show his support. He didn't know much about photography, but from what he'd seen of her work, he knew she had a real gift. She was able to combine her technical skill with an artistic eye to create incredibly compelling shots that drew the viewer in.

Now he sat in the ready room with the rest of his squadron, knowing he wouldn't get much sleep tonight. He'd have to cancel dinner with his architect, since he'd be staying late prepping for tomorrow's departure. The level of excitement in the ready room—a sort of lounge area where the pilots could just hang out and relax until their next flight—was palpable.

As the squadron commander detailed the mission, Jack looked around the room at the men in his unit. He'd flown or otherwise worked with most of them for years, and considered them all friends. Right now, they were all anticipating this new assignment. It might not be a combat mission, but it was a huge departure from the exercises they performed in the skies over Whidbey Island.

He glanced beside him to where Will sat, listening intently. Will loved flying, and Jack couldn't help feeling like a fraud because he didn't share the other man's obvious enthusiasm. Feeling Jack's eyes on him, Will turned and gave him a subtle thumbs-up.

"Man, this is great," he whispered, leaning toward Jack. "I didn't think we'd find ourselves on a carrier for at least another three or four months."

The *USS Ronald Reagan* was returning to its home port in San Diego, and the navy was going to take full advantage of the time spent cruising off the Pacific coast. While it was at sea, Jack's squadron would use it to hone their flying skills.

Jack knew he should be excited—and there was a part of him that definitely was—but not the way he would have been just a few short weeks ago. And that's what bothered him the most. He returned Will's thumbs-up, but even he knew it lacked enthusiasm.

"Hey, what's wrong?" Will asked.

Jack shook his head and tried to look motivated. "Nothing. It'll be great."

"Damn straight."

But Jack was aware that Will continued to give him sidelong looks throughout the remainder of the briefing. When the briefing was over, Jack grabbed his planner and followed the other pilots out of the ready room, hoping to avoid Will. He could fool most people, but Will knew him better than any of the other guys in the squadron. Sure enough, the other man fell into step beside him, and Jack could see he wasn't going to be allowed to just leave it alone.

"What's up with you? You're acting like you've just been grounded, not asked to fly to California and spend a couple of days playing on a carrier. I don't get it."

"Forget it," Jack said tersely. "You wouldn't understand, and I'm not going to explain it to you."

No way was he going to try and describe to Will how he was feeling right now. Will didn't have a wife or even a serious girlfriend. He'd made it clear that as long as he was a pilot, his flying came first. He always had women he could call for a good time, but he'd never committed himself to any of them. Jack had been like that when he'd been younger—when he'd been fairly new to flying and had been overly impressed with himself. But he realized he'd moved away from that kind of lifestyle. Maybe he was getting old, but the thought of banging some chick that he barely knew simply because she had a nice rack and was available no longer appealed to him. When he thought of the kind of woman he did want to be with, he saw Maggie's face. He liked the kind of man he was when he was with her.

They had reached the pilot's shack where he and Will each had a desk. Although, they rarely used them unless assigned as the squadron duty officer for the day, which entailed manning a desk and answering inane phone calls. Now the small office space was empty.

"Does this have anything to do with Maggie?" Will

asked. "I mean, it's fine if it does, but you need to get your head in the game."

"I'm fine," Jack growled, tossing his hat onto the desk and throwing himself into the chair. But when Will left him alone in the small office, he bent his head into his hands and silently acknowledged he was far from fine. He was, in fact, completely screwed up.

14

MAGGIE WAS UP early the following morning, and her first instinct was to peek out her bedroom window at the cottage.

"Damn it," she muttered, seeing that Jack's Land Rover was already gone. Did the man ever sleep? She'd gone to bed, exhausted, at ten o'clock, and he hadn't yet returned to the cottage. Now here it was barely six o'clock, and he'd already left.

Sighing, she took a quick shower and dressed in white shorts with a green tank top and a matching pair of green sandals. On impulse, she borrowed a floral scarf from Danielle and used it as a headband to keep her hair out of her face. She didn't know if she would see Jack today or not, but wanted to look nice for him in case he decided to make an appearance at the festival. Running lightly downstairs, she made herself a cup of coffee and checked her cell phone for messages. There was one, from Jack, from the previous night. He must have called right after she went to bed, and now she kicked herself for not staying up to wait for him. But as she listened to the message, a nagging sense of unease gripped her. There wasn't anything in his words to indicate anything was wrong, only that something had come up and he needed to talk with her.

Setting her coffee mug down on the counter, she quickly punched in his number and waited impatiently until he answered.

"Callahan."

"Jack, it's me. Maggie."

"Oh, hey." His voice grew warm. Intimate. Maggie could actually see him smiling. "How are you? I missed you last night."

"Mmm. I missed you, too. I tried to wait up for you, but by ten o'clock, I couldn't keep my eyes open anymore."

"Nah, I'm glad you didn't wait," he said. "I didn't get home until after eleven, and I needed to head out first thing this morning. I know you have a busy day today, so I definitely didn't want to disturb you."

"Oh." Maggie paused. "You said you needed to talk to me?"

She willed her racing heart to slow down. This didn't have to be bad news, she told herself. Sometimes people wanted to talk to you because they had good news. Or because they simply missed you, not because they wanted to destroy your world.

"Uh, yeah. I did want to talk to you." Jack's voice sounded so cautious that Maggie's imagination immediately jumped to conclusions. She held her breath. No matter what he said, she wouldn't cry. "Listen, sweetheart, I won't be able to see you for a few days. My squadron is flying to California to conduct some carrier exercises."

Whatever Maggie had expected him to say, that

wasn't it, and she felt the air leave her lungs in a re-lieved *whoosh*.

"Okay, that's fine," she assured him. "When do you leave?"

"Today, actually. We just found out yesterday, or I would have said something sooner. I'm sorry."

"No, no, it's okay. Trust me, I understand how the military works. You guys aren't in control of your own destinies. I get it." She drew in a deep breath. "So when will you be back?"

"I should return on Tuesday, definitely by Wednes-day."

"Wow. That's a long flight for just a few days."

"Not when you're flying at six hundred miles per hour," he said, and she could hear the grin in his voice.

Maggie felt herself smiling in return. "Will I see you before you leave?"

He hesitated. "Unlikely. My gear is already stowed in the aircraft, and we're going wheels up before noon."

"I understand. I'm not sure how this works, but do they let family and friends come onto the base to see your squadron off and say good-bye?"

"They do if it's for a long sea deployment, like six months, but not for one that only lasts a couple of days. I'll try to give you a call tonight, okay?"

"Okay. Fly safe, Jack."

"I always do. Be good," he said. "I'll be home be-fore you know it."

He hung up, and Maggie stood holding the phone in her hands, going over their conversation again in her head. He was leaving, but only for a couple of days. He'd said he would be back no later than Wednesday, but she missed him already. Unbidden, she thought of Phillip, when he'd told her he would be deployed for six months, but it had all been a lie. She'd never confronted him about that, and she wondered now if that might not be the reason why she'd had such a tough time putting it behind her. She'd simply walked away, refusing to talk to him or to hear his side of the story. She'd believed he'd been deployed, but in actuality he'd been off getting married to another woman.

She'd been so naive.

She had no idea when he'd been planning to tell her. Maybe he'd hoped to keep both a wife and a girlfriend. She knew there were guys out there who managed to do just that, but she'd never thought it would be the guy she was in love with.

Had been in love with.

Any feelings she might have had for Phillip Woodman had been destroyed that afternoon in the squadron commander's office. Giving herself a mental shake, she told herself she wouldn't think about that anymore. It no longer mattered. As Jack had told her, it was in her past. She had the future to think about now. Maybe a future with Jack, if she hadn't misread him.

Glancing at her watch, she realized she needed to scoot if she was going to make it to the shop before it opened and help Carly with the last-minute setup. She'd already decided to walk to Coupeville, as parking would be extremely limited and she didn't want to get hung up in any traffic jams. The walk was invigorating, taking her along the shores of Penn Cove and past the floating mussel farms. Seagulls wheeled and shrieked overhead, and Maggie kept an eye out for harbor seals, identifiable only by their small, dark heads bobbing in the waters. All in all, she decided, as she reached the outskirts of Coupeville, life was very good, and she had so much to be thankful for.

THE ARTS-AND-CRAFTS festival was chaotic and loud and bustling, and Maggie loved every minute of it. She recalled all the years she'd spent as a child helping her mother prepare for the festival, and how her mother had always let her place her own artwork up for sale, as amateurish as it had been. Maggie had loved the frenzy of getting ready, the people-watching and wheedling money out of her mother or her grandparents—usually both—for a sticky treat from one of the food vendors.

Today was no different, except that her mother wasn't there, and Maggie had decided to resist temptation and not sample any of the delicious food, despite the aromas that wafted through the streets. She was surprised and gratified to have sold three of her photographs within the first few hours of the festival, although she would have been content with the many compliments she received for her work.

"You see?" Carly had beamed in satisfaction. "I told you that you had a gift. My prediction is that you'll sell out well before the end of the festival."

Maggie didn't know if that was true, but she certainly hoped it was. Despite how busy she was, she found herself continually looking at her watch, wondering if Jack had left yet. She didn't think she would see the jets leave unless the pilots did a deliberate flyover of Coupeville, and she knew they were restricted from doing so.

It was getting close to noon when she looked over and saw Carly looking a little wilted and frazzled. She had to remind herself that the other woman was in her fifties, and despite the fact she seemed to have the energy of a woman half her age, she'd taken on a lot of responsibility since Eric had left.

"Carly, you look as if you could use a break," she

said during a lull, when the tent was nearly empty of customers. "Why don't you go get something to eat and sit in the shop for a little bit? At least it's air-conditioned in there."

"Oh, no, I'm absolutely fine," Carly protested, but when Maggie simply continued to look at her, the older woman's shoulders sagged. "Okay, you're right. I could use a break. I almost forgot how crazy these fairs can be, and I didn't get much sleep last night. But are you sure you can handle it?"

Maggie swept an arm around the now empty tent. "I'm sure. I'm just going to sit on this stool and smile. If any good-looking men come into the shop looking for me, you know where to send them."

"I sure do," Carly said, giving her a wink. Maggie watched the other woman until she disappeared into the shop, and then pulled out the paperback she'd tucked into her tote bag just in case business was slow. Several tourists meandered into the tent, but left again without buying anything. Nearly thirty minutes later, she heard her name being called and looked up to see the girl they had hired to help out in the shop. Maggie recalled her name was Wendy, and now she gave her an expectant smile.

"There's a man here to see you," she said shyly, and indicated someone who was just out of Maggie's sight, beyond the wall of the tent.

Jack.

Maybe his assignment had been canceled, or delayed. Maggie jumped down from the stool and waited expectantly, but the man who stepped into the tent was the last man she'd ever expected to see. Not Jack.

Phillip.

For an instant, her heart stopped beating and then

exploded into frenzied action inside her chest. She couldn't breathe, couldn't move, couldn't think. She could only stare at him, slack-jawed and speechless, wondering if she was in some horrible dream. Then he stepped toward her.

"Maggie."

She stepped back, putting the stool between them and looking beyond him to the shop, where surely Carly would come to her rescue at any moment. She didn't want to see this man, didn't want to speak to him, didn't want anything to do with him.

Seeing her recoil, he stopped and simply stood there, staring at her. "Maggie," he said again. "Nathan Stone called me to tell me you were back. I couldn't believe it. I know I shouldn't have come, but I had to see you for myself."

Maggie's breathing was uneven and shallow, and her palms were damp with perspiration. She felt light-headed, and even knowing it was a natural response to the shock she felt at seeing him, she couldn't seem to get a grip on herself. Slowly, she drew in several deep breaths, and he shifted back into focus. Maggie forced herself to look at him.

The years had been good to Phillip Woodman. His eyes were the same incredible blue that she recalled from that distant summer, and when he smiled at her, his teeth were still even and white. But she realized her knees weren't trembling beneath the force of that smile, and if her heart was still beating frantically, it was more from a sense of panic than anything else.

"Phillip," she said weakly. "I wasn't expecting to see you here. I didn't even know you were still in the area."

He gave her a sad smile. "Didn't you?"

Upon closer inspection, she saw the subtle signs that

the past ten years had left on him; his blond hair was thinner, and while still slim, she detected a slight thickening around his middle. There were creases around his eyes, and deep laugh lines on either side of his mouth.

"What are you doing here?" She looked around, hoping for an escape, but there was none.

"I had to come, Maggie." He took a step closer. "I'll never forgive myself for what happened between us. I've spent ten years wanting to explain to you what happened, why I married Pam." He stopped, as if searching for his next words. "Why I had to marry Pam."

Maggie blew out a hard breath, wishing the ground would open up and swallow her. Wishing the ground would open up and swallow him. "It doesn't matter, Phillip. It happened a long time ago, and I've moved on." She forced herself to smile at him. "Whatever happened, I forgive you."

Carly chose that moment to reenter the tent, looking curiously at Phillip as she did so. He was wearing khaki cargo shorts and a golf shirt, and except for his extraordinary eyes, he looked like a hundred other men at the fair. Carly obviously had no idea who he was, and there was no way Maggie was going to introduce them. To her horror, Phillip stepped back and made a gesture toward the street, where throngs of tourists were strolling from tent to tent.

"Do you want to take a walk?" he asked, smiling. "I could buy us an ice cream. It would be like old times."

Maggie tried not scowl. "No, thanks. I promised I would help with the festival, and I really shouldn't leave."

"Nonsense," said Carly, beaming at Phillip. "She could use a break, and she hasn't seen any of her old friends since she's been home. Go and get an ice cream, and I'll watch the tent."

When Maggie gave her a warning look, Carly either didn't notice or chose to ignore it, shooing her out of the tent as if she was still a child.

"Fine," she said ungraciously. "*Phillip* and I will be over at the Jolly Roger, getting a cone."

She had only a second to register the name recognition on Carly's face, followed immediately by an expression of horror, before Phillip ushered her out of the tent. Reluctantly, Maggie fell into step beside him. As the crowds jostled her, he put a hand at the small of her back to guide her. Maggie stiffened at the contact, but he didn't seem to notice.

"You can't imagine how many times I've thought of you over the years," he was saying. "I never had an opportunity to tell you how sorry I was, so when Nathan told me you were here, I had to come see you."

Now that she had recovered from the shock of seeing him, Maggie found herself feeling oddly detached, as if she was outside her body watching the awkward interaction of two strangers. She found she could talk to him—even ask him questions—without really caring what he said in return. They had reached the ice-cream shop, and they stood in line at the window, waiting to order.

"Where are you living now?" she asked.

"After I got out of the military, Pam and I bought a house in Port Townsend." He actually blushed, as if admitting that he and his wife had bought a house was somehow taboo. Maggie could not have cared less.

"You got out of the military?"

Phillip nodded. "Yes. They wanted to send me to Iraq, and, well, obviously I couldn't go. Not with a baby on the way."

He had a child. But of course he would. He'd been married for almost ten years. Naturally he and his wife would have had children.

"No," murmured Maggie, "obviously not."

They had reached the window, and Phillip ordered a butter-pecan cone for himself and a watermelon sherbet for Maggie, and then immediately looked alarmed. "That is still your favorite flavor, isn't it?"

Maggie nodded, wishing she could tell him no, that she no longer had a favorite anything from that summer she'd spent with him. But she did love watermelon sherbet, and the Jolly Roger made the best ice cream on the island, so she accepted the cone. They continued to walk along the sidewalk until they reached a set of wooden stairs that wound down between two shops to the beach behind the buildings. It had always been a favorite destination, and Maggie found her footsteps following the familiar steps as if ten years hadn't passed. They walked to the edge of the water where it lapped gently against the sand, and stood eating their ice cream but not saying anything.

Finally, having devoured the last bit of cone, Maggie wiped her lips and turned to Phillip. "Why are you here, Phillip? What did you possibly hope to gain by coming to see me today?"

Phillip looked at her, and Maggie was shocked to see real pain in his eyes. "I really did love you, Maggie. I just wanted you to know that, and it killed me to lie to you about the deployment."

"Then why did you?"

He made a helpless gesture. "Because I was a coward. Because I had no choice about getting married."

Maggie narrowed her eyes. "What do you mean? Everyone has a choice about getting married, Phillip."

He shifted uncomfortably and stared out over the water. "Not me."

Maggie waited, curious in spite of herself. When he finally looked back at her, his eyes were filled with regret and apology.

"I met Pam Kinney while I was stationed at Pearl Harbor, before I ever came to Whidbey Island. Before I ever met you."

Maggie's mouth opened in surprise.

"We didn't really know each other," Phillip continued, "but she was beautiful and fun, and made it clear that she liked to have a good time. I spent one crazy night with her in Hawaii during a navy ball, and then I flew out two days later. I never expected to see her again. I didn't even remember her name until her father showed up at Whidbey Island wanting to cut off my balls." He gave a bitter laugh. "Do you know what it's like to have a navy admiral gunning for your family jewels?"

Maggie's mouth fell open in sudden understanding. "She was pregnant."

"Yep. I had no idea, Maggie, I swear."

Covering her mouth with one hand, Maggie turned away. Before he'd ever met her, Phillip had gotten another woman pregnant. The knowledge shocked her. Whatever she'd expected him to say, it hadn't been that. She tried to imagine what it would have been like to have an irate admiral show up at your office and demand that you marry his daughter. She could almost feel pity for Phillip and what he must have gone through.

Turning back to him, Maggie forced herself to remain aloof. "That still doesn't explain why you lied to me."

"I was hoping to fix things, to make Pam understand

that I couldn't marry her, that maybe she shouldn't go through with the pregnancy. *I wanted to marry you.*"

His voice was so earnest that Maggie was taken aback. "You should have told me, Phillip. I would have been heartbroken, but I would have understood."

He made a groaning sound of sheer frustration. "You don't think I've beaten myself up for that a million times over the past ten years? After you left, I tried to get in touch with you, but nobody would tell me how to reach you. Not your mother or your brother. Not your friends. Nobody. It was like they circled the wagons and nobody was getting through. Especially not me."

Maggie smiled a little at the picture he'd created for her. She could just envision her family in all their outrage, determined to protect her from Phillip.

"So all you want is my forgiveness?" she asked.

He swallowed hard. "Yes. That's all I want. That, and to hear you say that I didn't completely fuck up your life. I knew how much you loved this place, and I always felt guilty for running you off."

Maggie frowned, his words disturbing to her. She *had* loved Whidbey Island, and if it hadn't been for Phillip, she might never have left. But she'd come back, and she'd found Jack. And she realized the rest of it didn't matter. Now, knowing the truth, she could feel only pity for Phillip, and for the woman he'd married. She'd spent the past ten years believing she was the victim. Now she wondered if she hadn't been the lucky one.

"I forgive you," she said, and realized she meant it. "And no, you didn't completely screw up my life. I mean, I was in therapy for a few years, but I got over it."

Phillip looked stricken. "Seriously?"

"Completely."

"I'm sorry, Maggie. Really sorry."

Maggie shrugged. "Like I said, it was a long time ago. We're different people now." She risked a glance at him. "So what did you have…a boy or a girl?"

Maggie was astonished by the change in Phillip at the mention of his child. His face softened and his smile was one of pure pride. "We had a little girl. And then a boy. And then another girl. My youngest is two years old."

Reaching into his pocket, he withdrew a wallet and flipped it open. An accordion of plastic photo-holders fell open, and there was his whole life for Maggie to see. She had thought the evidence of his marriage would hurt her, but instead, she felt a sense of relief. He was happy. He loved his family. She admired the photos of the three children, all of them blond and blue-eyed, and then fingered a photo of Phillip with a pretty, fair-haired woman.

"Is that her? Pam? She's beautiful."

"Yes. That's my wife."

Maggie glanced at his face, but he was absorbed in the picture. His face was so tender that Maggie's mouth fell open. "You really love her, don't you?"

When he looked at Maggie, she saw his eyes were suspiciously moist, but he gave a self-conscious laugh and closed the wallet. "Yeah, I really do. I love her so much. She's given me three beautiful kids, and we have a great life together. I didn't think we were going to make it at first, but she was determined. She was going to make it work or die trying."

Maggie reached out and laid a hand on his arm. "I'm really happy for you, Phillip."

He gave her a grateful smile. "You know what the kicker is? All these years, I've always wondered if you were the one I was really supposed to be with. I think I always questioned whether I really loved Pam, because in the back of my head there was always you. The girl who got away."

Maggie stared at him. "And now? Now that you've seen me and have had your chance to explain?"

Phillip looked chagrined. "Don't take this the wrong way, but I think things worked out for the best. I'm with the person I'm supposed to be with."

"Does she know you're here?"

He shook his head. "No. It would kill her if she knew I came to see you. I think she's always wondered if I really love her, or if given the choice, I'd rather be with you."

"You need to go home and be with your family, Phillip. You need to make sure that Pam has no doubts about how you feel about her. Tell her. Make sure she understands that if you could go back and do it all again, you'd still choose her."

"I will. I promise."

Turning toward her, he put his hands on her shoulders and searched her eyes. Maggie smiled, feeling generous and inexplicably warm toward this man whom she once believed had ruined her life. He'd done the right thing—the honorable thing. He'd committed himself to Pam, and he was obviously a doting dad and a good husband.

"Thank you, Maggie," he said softly. "It was really great seeing you."

Maggie nodded, feeling a lump form in her throat. "Yes. You, too."

She knew she wouldn't see him again, and she was so grateful that he had sought her out, and so grateful that she no longer loved him, that she stepped into his arms and hugged him tight. When he wrapped his arms around her and turned his face to kiss her, she didn't object. The kiss was one of farewell, and there was no passion in it, only the sweet finality of two people who had once shared so much.

When Maggie stepped back, she put a hand to his jaw and smiled at him. "Thank you, Phillip."

Before he could respond, a movement at the top of the wooden stairs that led to the sidewalk caught her attention. She turned to look, shading her eyes against the glare of the sun. There, standing on the top step in his flight suit, was Jack, with Carly on the sidewalk behind him wearing an expression of horror on her face. For one instant, her gaze collided with Jack's, and Maggie realized how incriminating the scene must look.

"Jack, wait," she called, but he had already reached the sidewalk, and as Maggie sprinted across the sand and up the steep staircase, he was gone, swallowed up in the throngs of people.

"What did he say?" she asked Carly, clutching the other woman's arm as her eyes frantically searched the crowds.

"He showed up at the shop pretty anxious to see you. He asked where you were, and I told him you'd gone to get an ice cream. So we followed you here, and at first we didn't see you. He wanted to know who the other guy was, so I told him. He looked like he wanted to be sick when he saw the two of you on the beach." Carly's face twisted in sympathy. "I'm sorry, hon, but what were you thinking?"

Maggie reached for her cell phone, only to realize she'd left it back at the tent. She gave Carly a helpless smile, even as tears threatened to blur her vision. "I was thinking that the best thing that ever happened to me was getting ditched by Phillip Woodman."

15

WILL WAS RIGHT; Jack needed to get his head in the game, but all he could see was Maggie, in another man's arms.

Kissing the bastard. Looking like she belonged there.

He was such an idiot.

When he'd learned that his departure had been pushed back by a couple of hours, he realized he had just enough time to drive out to Coupeville to see Maggie and say good-bye. He *needed* to see her. The phone call that morning had left him feeling unsatisfied.

He'd stopped at the cottage just long enough to ditch the Land Rover and grab his motorcycle. If there was traffic around the festival, he'd have a better chance of getting around it on the bike. He'd parked as close to the shop as he could and had drawn more than a few curious stares as he'd jogged through the crowds in his flight suit, impatient to reach Maggie. But when he'd arrived at the shop, she hadn't been there. The teenager at the register told him he would find Maggie in the tent, located on the corner. But when he'd reached the tent, only Carly had been inside. He'd known immediately that something was wrong by the distressed expression on her face as she'd told him that Maggie had gone for an ice-cream cone with a friend.

He'd known exactly who Phillip was the second Carly had told him the other man's name. It had taken every ounce of restraint he possessed not to go down to the beach and haul Maggie away from the guy, and then beat the living shit out of him. He'd been too aware that he was already pushing the limits for when he needed to be back at the air base, and the last thing he needed was to engage in a very public altercation that could get him grounded. It hadn't been easy, but some last vestige of sanity had allowed him to turn and walk away.

He'd been vaguely aware of Maggie calling his name, but he hadn't stopped. He hadn't trusted his own reaction if she'd told him that she was still in love with that bastard. His heart had been racing and his emotions had been churning.

He'd climbed onto his motorcycle and made the return trip to Oak Harbor too fast, hardly aware of what he was doing. All he could see was the expression on her face when she'd turned to see him standing there.

Shock.

Horror.

She clearly hadn't been expecting to see him, and he wondered when she'd contacted Phillip. Had she called him that morning, after she'd learned he would be gone for several days? She hadn't even had the decency to wait for him to leave before she'd put the moves on another guy. He understood that Maggie had a history with the bastard, but he'd have staked his life on the fact that she was falling for *him*. He thought he could forgive her just about anything, but he didn't think he could forgive her for cheating. Even knowing how he felt about commitment and infidelity, she'd chosen to

renew her relationship with Woodman—a man who
might still be married. Jack still felt sick every time he
thought about the kiss that he'd witnessed, which was
practically every second of every day.

That had been three days ago, and now he was cool-
ing his heels in the ready room of the *USS Ronald Reagan* as it slowly churned toward the west coast. After
they'd left Whidbey Island, Jack's squadron had flown
south, following the coastline to Los Angeles, until
they'd turned sharply inland toward Naval Air Station
Lemoore in California. They'd refueled and had hun-
kered down in the officer's quarters for the night. But
Jack hadn't slept. He'd spent most of the night thinking
about Maggie and trying to decide what to do. She'd
tried to call his cell phone, and had left a half-dozen
messages on his voice mail, but Jack hadn't listened to
any of them. He didn't have the courage or strength to
listen to her tell him that it was over between them—
that they were through.

In the morning they performed one last check of the
aircraft, and then departed to intercept the *USS Ronald
Reagan* in the waters of the north Pacific. One by one,
he and the rest of his squadron had landed their jets on
the deck of the enormous aircraft carrier, and had spent
the following day practicing their catapult takeoffs and
tail-hook landings. Now, after a long day of exercises
and postflight ops, he and the other pilots were kicking
back in the ready room, watching the news and playing
cards. It was nearly ten o'clock, but Jack wasn't ready
to call it a night.

He pulled his cell phone out, but there was no signal
in the middle of the Pacific. He wished now that he'd listened to Maggie's messages while he'd had the chance.
Ship-to-shore phone calls were possible, but even as he

considered the option, he quickly discarded it. He was a complete coward, because he didn't know if he could handle her telling him that she'd reconciled with her ex-fiancé. Besides, with ship-to-shore calls, the only guarantee was a complete lack of privacy, and he didn't need an audience for what he had to say to Maggie.

He looked over at the table next to him, where Commander Craig was leaning forward, playing with an electronic tablet and nursing a soda. Pushing his chair back, Jack stood up and walked over to the other table. The commander leaned back and nodded to him, indicating one of the empty chairs.

"Have a seat, Mick."

Jack sat down and gestured toward the tablet. "I don't want to disturb you."

"Nah, I'm just goofing around with some game that my kid got me hooked on." He shut the tablet down and pushed it aside. "You ready for tomorrow?"

"To head back to Whidbey?" Jack shrugged. "Sure."

"You performed some nice recoveries today. We'll do one more in the morning before we depart. I know you have over seventy-five carrier landings, and you're considered to be something of an expert, but I admire how you approach each one as if it's the first. You don't get cavalier about it."

"Believe me, sir," Jack replied, with feeling, "I'm way past the point in my life where I'm cavalier about anything."

"Call me Ben. So, what's on your mind?"

"You recall the other day when we were walking back to the ops shack, and you told me a story you'd heard about Eric Copeland's sister having been jilted?"

"Oh, yeah. That's right. For Admiral Kinney's daughter." The commander shrugged. "What about it?"

Jack hesitated. "Well, I'm crazy about her."

Ben's eyebrows shot up. "About the admiral's daughter?"

Jack laughed. "No, sir. About Eric's sister, Maggie. The girl who got jilted. But I need to find out…is the admiral's daughter still married to the guy? I mean, are they still together?"

Ben shrugged. "I have no idea. I don't pay much attention to that kind of stuff, as long as it doesn't involve me." He held up a finger as he reached for the tablet. "But I can find out. My wife knows everything."

"That's not necessary," Jack protested, but it was too late. The commander was already typing an email to his wife.

"I don't know when she'll receive this, but as soon as I hear back from her, I'll let you know." He tipped his head to one side as he considered Jack. "What's going on?"

Jack hesitated, and then leaned forward, lowering his voice. He needed some objective advice, and he knew he wouldn't get that from Will, no matter how well-meaning the other man was. Will still enjoyed one-time hook ups and hadn't had a serious relationship in his life. "I drove out to Coupeville the other day to say good-bye to my girl and found her on the beach with her ex-fiancé."

"The same guy who ditched her for the admiral's daughter?"

Jack compressed his lips. "Yeah."

"Maybe it was completely innocent, a chance encounter. Did you talk to her about it?"

"They were kissing, and it looked pretty intense. I left without speaking to her."

"Whoa." Ben sat back in his chair and rubbed the

back of his neck. "You didn't beat the shit out of the guy?"

Jack gave him a telling look.

"Yeah, I understand," Ben said. "But again, maybe the kiss wasn't what it appeared."

Jack blew out a hard breath. "I've been trying to convince myself of that since I left, and I wish now that I'd at least talked to her, but I didn't trust myself not to do something completely insane."

"So why do you want to know if the little prick is still married to the admiral's daughter?"

Jack scrubbed his hands over his face and then put his palms down on the table, his voice deadly serious. "Because if he's no longer married, and Maggie really wants to be with him, then I won't stand in their way. But if he is married, and he's just messing around with her, then God help him. He won't live to break her heart twice." Standing up, he shook the other man's hand. "Thanks."

"Glad to help. Good luck."

But as Jack made his way through the ship to one of the lower decks, where he and the other guys in the squadron had been provided sleeping berths, he knew he'd need more than luck on his side. He just hoped he wasn't too late.

THE SUN WAS low in the sky when Jack finally saw Whidbey Island come into view in the distance. They had returned to San Diego aboard the *USS Ronald Reagan* that morning and had performed several flyovers of the port, much to the delight of the families who had gathered near the docks to welcome their sailors home after an extended sea deployment. They'd made one quick refueling stop in northern California, and now that Jack could see Whidbey Island, he was anxious to get on the ground and get home.

He listened through his headset as Will provided the coordinates and position for their landing. They circled out over the open water as they waited their turn to land, and as Jack looked out through the glass canopy of the cockpit at the waters below, he spotted a pod of whales swimming off the northern tip of the island. He smiled, recalling the night he had met Maggie.

"Hey, Robot," he said to Will through the headset, "check out the water at nine o'clock."

"Oh, man, that's beautiful," crooned Will. "Better than SeaWorld! I'll bet there are nine of them in that pod."

"At least. Okay, here we go."

They had been cleared for landing, and now Jack circled back around to line up with the airstrip. He throttled back as he released the landing gear, and in mere seconds, they were touching down and screaming along the tarmac until Jack applied the brakes and began to power down.

"Nice landing, Mick," Will said.

"It's good to be back," Jack replied. He'd only been gone for four days, but he felt like it had been forever. He taxied the jet along the airstrip to the hangar area, where a group of maintenance technicians immediately began climbing over the aircraft.

Jack raised the canopy, levered himself out of the cockpit and climbed down the side of the jet. Commander Craig was already there, waiting on the tarmac. Pulling his sunglasses out of his pocket, Jack slid them on and nodded to the other man, who held up a smart phone.

"I asked my wife if they were still married, and she just replied."

Jack waited. "And?"

Ben grinned. "Not only married, but by all accounts very happy."

The news should have made Jack relieved, but now he knew the bastard was only using Maggie, and she probably had no idea. She had a soft heart, and would buy whatever bag of horseshit he was selling to her. As Ben strolled toward the hangar, Jack hung back to wait for Will, but noticed the other man's attention was fixed somewhere behind Jack. Turning to look, Jack stilled.

A small group of people stood beside the base ops building, including the base commander, Captain Beauchamp, a tall man with a balding head and a gaze that could freeze ice. Jack had never had any issues with him, and he wanted to keep it that way. Standing beside the captain was another officer whom Jack didn't recognize, although he had no trouble identifying the insignia on the man's uniform.

He was a navy admiral.

Immediately, Jack's thoughts flew to what he might have done wrong that would warrant this kind of welcome committee. He hadn't beaten the living hell out of Phillip Woodman, so it couldn't have anything to do with him. He hadn't crashed his jet, or performed any illegal maneuvers, or gotten into any brawls.

Will climbed down and stood beside him, his face reflecting his awe. "Jesus, man," he said beneath his breath, "what the hell did you do now? That's a freaking admiral over there."

"Maybe it's you he wants, and not me," Jack muttered, as they exchanged a look.

"Let's get this over with," the other man replied.

They walked toward the group, but before they were halfway across the tarmac, the admiral saluted Captain Beauchamp and then turned and walked toward a waiting vehicle, accompanied by his entourage of aides. As the admiral turned away, Jack saw a woman standing just behind him. It was Maggie, and his step nearly faltered. His heart began to hammer in his chest as he drank her in. She looked beautiful in a pretty floral dress with her hair blowing wild across her face.

"Since when did they begin letting civilians onto the air base?" Will asked beneath his breath. "She's not family, so what the hell is she doing here?"

"No idea." Jack dragged his gaze away from Maggie long enough to salute the base commander.

"Sir."

"Callahan, Robinson. Welcome back."

"Thank you, sir." Jack tried not to look at Maggie, but he was acutely conscious of her standing at his commander's side.

"In light of the recent exercise over the Pacific, I'm giving your squadron three days of liberal leave, starting now." His steely glance flicked between Jack and Maggie, and a ghost of a smile touched his lips. "I must be getting soft. Enjoy your time off, gentlemen."

He turned and spoke quietly to Maggie, before squeezing her arm and walking past them to intercept the other pilots who had just landed.

Will looked at Jack and grinned. "This is my cue to leave before he changes his mind. I'll stash your helmet for you and take care of the paperwork."

"Thanks." Jack handed Will his helmet, and then turned and looked at Maggie. She was watching him with a mixture of hope and apprehension on her face. Afraid he might actually reach out and haul her against his chest, he thrust his hands deep into the pockets of his flight suit. "How are you?"

He knew his voice was cool, and that he must appear remote, but until she told him that Phillip Woodman meant nothing to her, he wouldn't be able to relax.

She tucked her hair behind her ear, and then hugged herself around the middle. "I'm fine."

Clearly, she wasn't. He knew her well enough to see she was a complete bundle of nerves. "Why are you here?"

"To see you."

"How did you get onto the base without an escort?"

She colored. "I did have an escort."

Jack frowned. "Who?"

"Will you take off your sunglasses? I can't see your eyes."

"Who escorted you onto the base, Maggie?" Jack kept his mirrored glasses on; they were all the protection he had from her.

"Admiral Kinney."

Jack stared at her in dawning understanding. "Not *the* admiral? The one whose daughter ended up marrying your fiancé?"

Maggie compressed her lips and nodded in resignation. "Ex-fiancé. So you know the story, huh?"

"Kinda hard not to, babe, after seeing you on the beach with your tongue down her *husband's* throat."

She gasped in outrage at his mocking tone. "You don't know what you saw, and you didn't even have the decency to stick around long enough for me to explain!"

Looking around, Jack saw the other pilots beginning to cross the tarmac toward the hangar where they stood. He thought furiously for a moment, and then made a decision. "C'mon," he said, and took Maggie's arm, steering her through the hangar to the parking lot beyond.

"Where are we going?"

"I don't know," he growled. "Somewhere private. Anywhere but here."

But when they stopped in front of his motorcycle, he realized they had a problem. Maggie was wearing a dress. No way could she straddle a bike and maintain any modesty.

"It's fine," she said, reading his mind. "I can still ride. Do you have another helmet?"

He did, and he reached into the saddlebag to pull one out for her. A gust of wind blew her hair across her mouth and plastered her dress against her hips and thighs, leaving nothing to the imagination. Jack thrust the helmet at her and bent to pull his helmet out of the other saddlebag. "Did you drive over here? Maybe we can take your car."

"No, I didn't drive."

"Fine." Jerking his helmet on, he straddled the bike and released the kickstand. "Climb on."

He watched as Maggie fastened her helmet, and then tried to swing her leg over the seat without flashing him, but it was no good. He got an eyeful of smooth, slender thighs and a pair of pale pink panties that barely covered her. He groaned inwardly, knowing he was a goner. When she settled in behind him, with her bare thighs on either side of his, he couldn't prevent his body from responding.

"Hold on to me," he growled, and kicked the bike into gear, gratified when she flung her arms around his waist, hanging on for dear life. Through the thin material of his flight suit, he could feel her heat. Her breasts were squashed against his back, and her palms were flattened over his stomach. She clung to him like a spider monkey, and he loved it.

HE LEFT THE base and steered them north, toward Deception Pass, roaring along the coastal road with the wind in their faces. Maggie pressed her face against his back and breathed in his scent, her arms wound tightly around him. The ride was both exhilarating and frightening, because she didn't know what he intended to do or say once they reached their destination. She hated that she couldn't see his eyes behind the mirrored sunglasses, and so had no hint of what he might be thinking or feeling. But she took hope from the fact that she was with him now, holding him. Whatever he believed he'd seen that day on the beach, she'd make him understand the truth. For her, there was no other man but him.

When they reached the visitor's center at the Deception Pass bridge, he pulled into the parking lot.

"Why are we stopping here?" she asked in his ear, reluctant to release him.

"It seems appropriate," he answered cryptically, and dismounted, unfastening his helmet and hanging it from the handlebar. He held out a hand to Maggie, and he didn't look away when she clambered gracelessly off the bike, knowing she was giving him quite the peep show, but not caring. This time, he unfastened her helmet for her, and his fingers brushed against her cheeks. She drew in her breath and looked at him.

"Take your glasses off," she pleaded.

"Not yet." He looked at her feet, and she followed his gaze. She wore a pair of sandals with delicate straps, and immediately she knew that he had intended for them to hike down the steep trail to the beach where they had first met. Instead, he caught her hand and pulled her across the street, to a trail that had been a favorite of hers as a kid. It was wide and relatively flat, with only a mild incline.

"Goose Rock?" she asked in surprise, as she followed him. "You're taking me to the overlook?"

"I want you to see something," he said, not elaborating.

They passed two couples returning to the visitor's center, and Maggie didn't miss the curious looks they received. Before long, the path widened and leveled out, changing to a paved trail that led to a circular overlook surrounded by a low railing. They were at the highest point overlooking Deception Pass, with unobstructed views of the ocean and the treacherous strait that led to the narrow bay behind Whidbey Island.

Without releasing her hand, Jack drew her to the railing and pointed to a small waterfront community far below them. "That's Cornet Bay, where you first took a picture of me. My grandfather kept his boat on one of those docks." He angled his hand slightly. "See that knoll, just above the bay, where they've cleared out some trees?"

Maggie nodded, hoping he wouldn't notice how she leaned against him. Even with the railing, the height made her feel a little dizzy. Forcing herself to focus on where he was pointing, she could see the site had unobstructed views of both the small harbor and Deception Pass.

"That's the land my grandparents left to me, and where I'm building a house." He turned to Maggie. "I'm staying here on Whidbey Island, Maggie. I want you to stay with me. If you think you're still in love with that bastard—"

Maggie put her fingers over his mouth. "I'm not."

He pulled her hand away. "I saw you."

"No. He found out that I'd returned, and he came to the festival to apologize for what happened ten years ago. He doesn't love me. He has a wife and a family, and he's completely committed to them." She paused. "And I don't love him. Not even close. I knew that as soon as I saw him again."

"Why was his father-in-law at the air base with you?"

"When you saw us on the beach, we were just saying good-bye. I know it must have looked bad, but you left before I could explain. Phillip wanted to make amends, thinking he might have screwed up my life a second time." Maggie took his hand. "He called his father-in-law and asked him for a favor—to escort me onto the air base so that I could be there when you returned. He didn't want to give you the opportunity to walk away without at least talking to me." She frowned, unable to read his expression. "Now will you take those sunglasses off?"

Reaching up, he pulled them off, and Maggie felt her heart stutter at the raw emotion in his hazel eyes.

"Jesus, Maggie," he said, his voice rough. "You have no idea what I've been through these past four days, thinking you were back with him. I'd already decided I wasn't going to let you go without a fight."

Maggie put a hand on his chest and could feel the heavy, uneven thumping of his heart beneath her palm. "I'm not going anywhere, Jack. I'm staying here on Whidbey Island. If you want me…"

With a groan, Jack dragged her into his arms, and Maggie found herself surrounded by his heat and strength. "Want you?" he asked in a ragged voice. "Lady, since the night we met, I haven't thought about anything except how much I want you."

He cupped her face in his big hands and Maggie saw the love and the need in his hazel eyes, before he dipped his head and covered her mouth with his. The potency of the kiss made her knees go wobbly, and she leaned into him, returning his kiss with all the emotion that was in her heart.

When he finally pulled away, he bent his forehead to hers and stroked his thumbs over her cheeks. "You put me through hell, you know that? I've never felt so powerless before in my entire life, like I was spinning out of control and I couldn't even press the eject button to save myself."

Maggie's breath mingled with his as she gave a shaky laugh. "I hope I never give you reason to press that button."

With one last, hard kiss, Jack turned toward the spectacular view, wrapping his arms around Maggie so that her back was against his chest and his face was next to hers. Secure in his arms, Maggie found she could actually admire the view without the fear of falling.

"When I was flying in, Will and I saw a pod of orcas just off the north end of the island," he said in her ear. He pointed toward the narrow strait. "Look, there they are."

Following his finger, Maggie saw them. Two orcas were making their way through the narrow pass, toward the bay.

"Do you think they're the same two we saw that first night?" she asked, watching them.

"Maybe. I can't tell for sure from here, but it looks like a male and a female."

Maggie thought back to that first night, when the female had headed toward the open sea, leaving the male to swim alone toward the bay. Now she watched as the two swam beneath the soaring bridge, both of them heading into the bay. She smiled and angled her face to press a kiss against the corner of Jack's mouth, knowing she was finally where she was supposed to be.

Epilogue

Nine months later

MAGGIE STOOD ON the wide deck with her elbows braced on the railing, drinking in the view of Cornet Bay. Through the open doors behind her, she could hear one of the twins wailing plaintively, and she smiled. Probably Paige, since she seemed to always be hungry and wasn't shy about letting her parents know. Paige's twin brother, Josh, was much mellower, and Maggie could already see which one of them was going to be a handful. Even at seven months old, they had their own personalities. She breathed in the crisp, salty air and closed her eyes, feeling completely content.

"Hey, what are you thinking about?"

Opening her eyes, she turned and smiled at Jack. She hadn't heard him approach. He leaned on the railing beside her, cradling a beer in one hand, and watched her with warm eyes.

"I was just thinking how perfect this house is, and how you've managed to capture the best of the view and the light," she said, turning to look up at the soaring windows behind them.

The post-and-beam house had been completed less than a month ago, and Jack had finally moved out of the small cottage and into his new home. "I'm glad you approve," he said, grinning as he pulled her into his arms, "since it's your house, too. And I have you to thank for pulling it all together. I couldn't have done it without you. You make it feel like a real home."

Jack had done a three-month sea tour, and had returned just weeks before the house was completed. While he'd been gone, Maggie had helped to oversee the construction of the house, providing him with daily updates on the progress, since he couldn't be there himself. She'd been waiting for him on the base the day he'd returned from his deployment, and he'd proposed to her that night.

Now she slid her arms around his waist and pressed a lingering kiss against his mouth. "It is a real home. It's our home."

"Hey, you two, knock it off."

They turned to see Eric step onto the deck, a baby tucked in one arm, greedily sucking on a bottle. The twins were just over seven months old, and although they were both a little small, Maggie felt sure they would soon catch up. Paige was certainly doing her best, and Maggie reached out to stroke the infant's soft cheek.

"She is so perfect," she murmured, watching the baby. As if sensing she had an appreciative audience, Paige gave her a watery smile and gurgled, making them laugh.

"Maggie, can you take Josh for a minute? I want to show Danielle the necklaces I made while I was in California last month."

Maggie's mother, Valerie, stood in the doorway to

the kitchen, holding little Josh, while Danielle stood right behind her, looking tired but happy.

"Of course I'll take him," Maggie said, moving forward, but Jack was there before her.

"I've got him," he said, taking the baby from Valerie's arms with an easy confidence. Josh's eyes widened and he stared at Jack for a long, steady moment before reaching out one chubby hand toward his beer. "Not so fast, little man," Jack laughed, and handed his beer to Maggie. "Maybe when you're older, and your parents aren't standing right there."

"Yeah, okay, you're off my list of potential babysitters," Danielle called to him, but she was laughing as Valerie led her back into the house.

"Wow," Maggie murmured, watching Jack and her brother as they each held a baby. "Where's my camera when I need it? Nobody will believe this unless I capture it on film."

"Hey, no fair," Eric protested, easing himself into an Adirondack chair. "I'm always holding one of them."

"You're right," Maggie said in an indulgent tone. "You're a wonderful father."

She walked over to where Jack stood cuddling little Josh, looking completely comfortable in his role as future uncle. The baby had wrapped his fist around one of Jack's fingers and was watching Jack's face intently.

"Are you ready for this?" she asked.

He looked at her. "For what? Your whole family descending on us?"

"Well, that, too," she said, smiling. "No, I meant are you ready for *this*—a family?"

"That's why I gave you a ring," he said, catching her hand and lifting it to his mouth. The diamond solitaire on her finger sparkled in the sunlight. "Because I'm ready. I've been ready since the day I met you."

"Oh, Jack," she whispered, feeling herself go soft at the tender expression in his eyes. "I love you so much."

Leaning forward, he kissed her over the baby's head. "I love you, too."

"Do you think your grandparents would approve? Of the house? Of me?"

Jack smiled into her eyes. "Sweetheart, I know that wherever they are, they not only approve, they are absolutely ecstatic. We're both exactly where we should be. We're home."

Maggie leaned her head on his shoulder and looked out over the water, knowing it was true. She was exactly where she should be. Where she wanted to be. Forever.

* * * * *

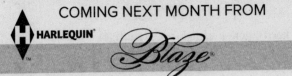
Available July 23, 2013

#759 THE HEART WON'T LIE • *Sons of Chance*
by Vicki Lewis Thompson

Western writer Michael James Hartford needs to learn how to act like a cowboy—fast. But it isn't until he comes to the Last Chance Ranch—and falls for socialite-turned-housekeeper Keri Fitzgerald—that he really discovers how to ride....

#760 TO THE LIMIT • *Uniformly Hot!*
by Jo Leigh

Air force pilot Sam Brody has had his wings clipped. Now he's only teaching other flyboys. And his fling with the hottest woman on the base has taken a nosedive, too...because Emma Lockwood belongs to someone else.

#761 HALF-HITCHED • *The Wrong Bed*
by Isabel Sharpe

Attending a destination wedding is the *perfect* time for Addie Sewell to seduce Kevin, The One Who Got Away. But when she climbs into the wrong bed and discovers sexy yacht owner Derek, The One Who's Here Right Now might just be the ticket!

#762 TAKING HIM DOWN
by Meg Maguire

Rising MMA star Rich Estrada loves exactly two things—his family and a good scrap. But when sexy Lindsey Tuttle works her way into his heart, keeping his priorities straight may just prove the toughest fight of his life.

SPECIAL EXCERPT FROM

HARLEQUIN®

Blaze®

Enjoy this sneak peek at

Half-Hitched

by Isabel Sharpe, part of The Wrong Bed series
from Harlequin Blaze

Available July 23 wherever
Harlequin books are sold.

Addie Sewell held her breath as she headed for Kevin's
room. *First bedroom on the right.*

Eleven years later, she'd feel that wonderful mouth on hers
again, would feel those strong arms around her, would feel his
hand on her breast. And so much more.

Addie reached for the handle and slipped into the room.
Done!

She closed the door carefully behind her, listening for any
sign that Kevin had heard her.

He was still, his breathing slow and even.

She was in.

For a few seconds Addie stood quietly, amazed that she'd
actually done this, that she, Princess Rut, had snuck mostly
naked into a man's room in order to seduce him.

A sudden calm came over her. This was right.

As silently as possible, she walked toward the bed. In the
dim light she could see a swathe of naked back, his head bent,
partly hidden by the pillow.

A rush of tenderness. Kevin Ames. The One That Got Away.

HBEXP79765

She let her sweater pool at her feet as she pictured Kevin hours earlier. Laughing with that Derek Bates and all the other wedding guests.

Totally naked now, heart pounding, she climbed onto the bed then slid down to spoon behind him. His body was warm against hers, his skin soft, his torso much broader than she'd expected. They fit together perfectly.

She knew the instant he woke up, when his body tensed beside hers.

"It's Addie."

"Addie," he whispered.

Addie smiled. She would have thought after all he had to drink and how soundly he'd been passed out downstairs, that she might have trouble waking him.

She drew her fingers down his powerful arm—strangely bigger than she expected. "Do you mind that I'm here?"

He chuckled, deep and low. Addie stilled. She'd *never* heard Kevin laugh like that.

Before she could think further, his body heaved over and she was underneath him, his broad masculine frame trapping her against the sheets. And before she could say anything, he kissed her, a long, slow sweet kiss.

When he came up for air, she knew she'd have to do something. *Say something.*

But then he was kissing her again. And this time her body caught fire.

Because it was so, so good.

Beyond good. Unbelievably good.

It just wasn't Kevin.

Pick up HALF-HITCHED by Isabel Sharpe, available July 23 wherever you buy Harlequin® Blaze® books.

HBEXP79765

REQUEST YOUR FREE BOOKS!
2 FREE NOVELS PLUS 2 FREE GIFTS!

HARLEQUIN

Blaze®

red-hot reads!

YES! Please send me 2 FREE Harlequin® Blaze™ novels and my 2 FREE gifts (gifts are worth about $10). After receiving them, if I don't wish to receive any more books, I can return the shipping statement marked "cancel." If I don't cancel, I will receive 4 brand-new novels every month and be billed just $4.74 per book in the U.S. or $4.96 per book in Canada. That's a savings of at least 14% off the cover price. It's quite a bargain. Shipping and handling is just 50¢ per book in the U.S. and 75¢ per book in Canada.* I understand that accepting the 2 free books and gifts places me under no obligation to buy anything. I can always return a shipment and cancel at any time. Even if I never buy another book, the two free books and gifts are mine to keep forever.

150/350 HDN F4WC

Name	(PLEASE PRINT)	
Address		Apt. #
City	State/Prov.	Zip/Postal Code

Signature (if under 18, a parent or guardian must sign)

Mail to the Harlequin® Reader Service:
IN U.S.A.: P.O. Box 1867, Buffalo, NY 14240-1867
IN CANADA: P.O. Box 609, Fort Erie, Ontario L2A 5X3

Want to try two free books from another line?
Call 1-800-873-8635 or visit www.ReaderService.com.

* Terms and prices subject to change without notice. Prices do not include applicable taxes. Sales tax applicable in N.Y. Canadian residents will be charged applicable taxes. Offer not valid in Quebec. This offer is limited to one order per household. Not valid for current subscribers to Harlequin Blaze books. All orders subject to credit approval. Credit or debit balances in a customer's account(s) may be offset by any other outstanding balance owed by or to the customer. Please allow 4 to 6 weeks for delivery. Offer available while quantities last.

Your Privacy—The Harlequin® Reader Service is committed to protecting your privacy. Our Privacy Policy is available online at www.ReaderService.com or upon request from the Harlequin Reader Service.

We make a portion of our mailing list available to reputable third parties that offer products we believe may interest you. If you prefer that we not exchange your name with third parties, or if you wish to clarify or modify your communication preferences, please visit us at www.ReaderService.com/consumerschoice or write to us at Harlequin Reader Service Preference Service, P.O. Box 9062, Buffalo, NY 14269. Include your complete name and address.

HB13R2